WICKED GAME

WICKED GAME
Copyright © 2021 Paul Anthony Werner

Cover Design and Typesetting by FormattingExperts.com

ISBN 978-0-578-92347-5
Published by NouvelleNoir Publishing
NouvelleNoir.com

PAUL ANTHONY WERNER

WICKED GAME

CHAPTER 1
ME

I want to begin by stating for the record that I feel very bad about how things turned out with Delilah. There were many people in Orange County who thought she was innocent, and God knows I told anyone who would listen that there was no way she was capable of murder.

I still pull her picture out, from time to time. Jesus, she was beautiful back then, and naturally I can never look at her image without reliving the brief moments of pleasure she gave me in bed.

The photo was taken on some nice person's splendid sailing ship, well before I met her. She stands gracefully arched from its mainmast, holding it with one hand and her other raised in a tentative and endearing little half-wave, as if she's uncertain the camera will really be shuttered. She wears a turquoise thong bikini, for which she has the perfect figure, a wide-brimmed sunhat and oversized sunglasses. She's a tiny little girl, barely five foot two, with an adorably pretty face and long sun-bleached hair. She's tan and been recently in the water. Sunlight playing on the moisture gives her skin an erotic sheen. She just looks so damn carefree and so naively happy that you want to pick her up and hug her.

Do I love her still? Did I ever? Always a tough question for a man to answer, isn't it, the line between love and lust being so damnably elusive?

The thing is, these sorts of decisions are very difficult. I mean the big ones, the life-changing irrevocable choices we sometimes are required to make. Sometimes situations arise that force us to choose between two good things, only one of which we can have. The ridiculous irony, of course, is that the one we pick in such circumstances becomes less dear in the having, while the one forgone invariably seems more valuable by its very absence. Sorting it all out is tough, particularly when issues such as capital crime are involved, or the attentions of a supremely desirable woman.

Either way, I can honestly say that I stuck with her to the bitter end.

1

CHAPTER 2
FRANCIS CAPELLA

Francis Capella was one of the most successful plaintiff attorneys in Orange County. It turns out he was also widely regarded as one of the biggest pricks in Orange County, and that's out of a very crowded field. Consequently the news of his spectacular death was received not only with the expected media hoopla, but also a fair amount of unrestrained celebration in certain quarters, for example by the scores of men he'd screwed over the years in divorce court.

The accident happened early on a Sunday morning in late February, the first dry day after a week of steady rain. It was witnessed by just one individual, a man who happened to be surfcasting on the beach in a cove just below the tight turn in the highway where Capella lost control of his vehicle, and was therefore able to watch as the attorney's new Porsche 911 Turbo coupe plunged over the cliff, what was moments before an expensive piece of German automotive machinery becoming an unguided missile consisting of steel, exotic metal alloys, premium leather, space age plastic and, unfortunately, one very terrified attorney.

By a tragic happenstance that would later become the subject of extended legal wrangling between the state of California and his estate, Capella managed to slip his car through a small gap in the guardrail created by a landslide during the recent downpours and left unrepaired by Caltrans.

Tough luck for him, of course, but the sweet sound of opportunity knocking for me, it turned out, as I received a call late the next day informing me that his life was insured by a company for which I occasionally do investigations, Pacific Life. They were looking at 2.5 million dollars, with an accidental death clause that would double the payoff unless it developed that somebody made the accident happen and I could prove it, in which case I'd be in line for a nice bonus.

I figured it was a long shot, but there were enough elements of the accident to maybe give pause to anyone of a suspicious nature. Nobody more congenitally suspicious than insurance executives, trust me.

My first move was to pick up the phone and make a lunch date with Mingee.

CHAPTER 3
NGUYEN MAI, AKA MINGEE

Nguyen Trihn Mai, Mingee to her friends, is probably the luckiest woman I know, despite the fact that she once dated yours truly. I say that because she dodged an economy-size bullet as a newborn baby, when she was being transported on the Air Force C-5 that crashed near Saigon in 1974 during Operation Babylift. It was the last crumbling days of the South Vietnamese government and Uncle Sam was pulling hundreds of friendly locals out, including orphans like Mai. Miraculously, she survived the accident, made it to the U.S., and was subsequently adopted and raised by a nice middle-aged couple in Mission Viejo. They were her second lucky break.

The Vietnamese fortunate enough to make it to the States came to be well-regarded for making the most of the opportunity, and not the least my Mingee. She worked hard and with the possible exception of the regrettable Patrick Brennan episode life in America's been very good to her, and vice versa.

Mai's mother was French-Vietnamese and her father an American GI, identity and address unknown. She got the best of all three cultures. She has long and straight black glossy hair, a slender figure and a sweet, soul-melting heart-shaped face.

We first met at a softball game when she was fresh out of the police academy, and we dated exclusively for a couple of years. If I'd had it in me, I would have married her when I had the chance and maybe made a bunch of Irish-French-Vietnamese babies. I didn't. And so she moved on. Nevertheless we remain good friends and I seek her out from time to time, partly for old times' sake and partly because she is one of the best cops I know and a well-placed contact with the Orange County Sheriff's Department.

So I invited her to lunch at her favorite place, Au Lac, a popular Vietnamese vegan restaurant in Fountain Valley. She drove down from the office in Santa Ana and met me in the early afternoon. We took a table in the back, as private a spot as possible, and spent a few moments exchanging small talk while looking over the menu, which is extensive. I ordered shredded tofu spring rolls and a traditional rice noodle pho. Mai went with the seaweed salad. We enjoyed a nice meal that passed with more small talk and me gazing into those big brown cat's eyes of hers, thinking about old times, but Mai could sense that this wasn't a social visit.

As we sipped on after-lunch cups of Vietnamese ice coffee, she said, "All right, Patrick. What's up? I know you didn't ask me here to take a stroll down memory lane. What's on your mind?"

I gave her a shy grin and said, "Okay, I confess. You always could read me."

"Yeah, I always could. That was the problem."

"Maybe so. Anyway, what's on my mind is the Capella thing."

"What thing would that be?"

"Don't be coy, darlin'. We've too much history, and here I've driven all the way to Little Saigon just for you. You know. Francis Capella. The late Francis Capella. Dude had a hot young wife with a fat insurance policy and probably a prenup in the mix to consider, not to mention a list of enemies about half the size of the Orange County white pages. You gonna tell me the Sheriff's department isn't looking into his death? His violent and untimely death? And by the way, it's not idle curiosity on my part. The insurer has me looking into the case."

She was nicely turned out in a businesslike cream-colored shirt and jacket, very short skirt, with a white linen blouse, and she turned sideways in her seat, crossed one lovely leg over the other for my edification, and smiled.

"Pat," she said, "we have a radical new policy in the department that we're experimenting with. We've decided to wait for a crime to be committed before we do a criminal investigation. What do you think?"

A pause for effect, and then, "The fact is you're right, Mr. Capella had a lot of enemies. A lot of people in Orange County are thrilled to see him dead. However, he also had what amounts to a street-legal racecar and a reputation as a lunatic behind the wheel. Besides which, there is absolutely no evidence of foul play. Therefore, they're calling it an accident all the way and I'm good with that. I wouldn't get your hopes up."

5

"Well, we'll see, won't we?"

"You know what they're saying around the office? A fool and his money are soon driving more car than he can handle."

"Is that what they're saying? Well, you are working with a group of comedic geniuses. Congratulations. Come on, Mai, don't do this to me. You *are* going to take a look, right?"

"Of course. It's a fatal vehicle accident, and a very high profile one at that. CHP intends to give the wreck a going over. They have an expert coming down from Sacramento. And of course that asshole Tanaka over in the PA's office has called. He's starting to breathe pretty heavy. He just finished up that child molester thing and he's looking around to see where his next trophy's coming from, so you're not the only one with suspicious thoughts bouncing around inside your pretty little head. But it's early days, lover. They're still working on getting the damn thing off the beach, the car I mean. They're going to need a crane. Be patient."

"Okay, okay. I guess it's a mess, the car?"

"You bet. Basically a smoldering black pile of compacted metal. They've more or less scraped his remains, what's left of them, from inside. Not a lot there, I can tell you. He was cremated by the blast and fire. Very ugly situation, the kind of thing that makes you glad you're not with the ME's office."

"Any chance of toxicology?"

"I really doubt it. Doesn't look like there's going to be any tissue to work with that hasn't been incinerated. Why, you figure he's out driving drunk on a Sunday morning?"

"Maybe. So who you dating?"

"Has it been that long since we caught up?"

"Six months I figure."

"He's with the department. You wouldn't know him."

"A cop? Say it ain't so, Mingee. Did I teach you nothing?"

"Unfortunately, Pat, you taught me quite a bit. And you?"

I shook my head. "I should have grabbed you when I had the chance."

"That's the truest thing I've heard come tumbling out of your mouth in a long time, my foolish friend."

A moment of awkward silence while we each contemplated the sad history of our affair from our respective perspectives, after which I said,

6

"Promise me one thing, Mai. If anything develops you'll keep me in the loop, all right? Nice payday for me if I can prove Capella's death was a setup."

"Sure, Pat."

"And I'm not going to step on any toes if I snoop around? I'll be talking to Mrs. Capella, naturally, being she's the beneficiary. Would the department have a problem if I visit the medical examiner, and maybe take a look at the wreckage after CHP's done, that sort of thing?"

"No problem. I'll square it."

"And the papers said there was a witness. Can I talk to him?"

"I'll get you his name and number. I'll ask him. As long as he's willing, we have no problem."

"Thanks a million, beautiful."

"Just catch the tab, sport. That'll be sufficient for now. It's been a treat."

Watching her walk away from me in the parking lot was an exercise in ambivalence, I'll tell you for nothing. On the one hand, Mai is one great combination package of brains and looks and I still carry a torch. On the other hand, I'm simply not the marrying kind.

CHAPTER 4

DELILAH

Delilah. Del. Sometimes, just D. Delightful. Delectable. Delovely.

The first time I laid eyes on her she was naked, or may as well have been, for all the cover her scandalous little outfit provided.

She lay atop an expensive-looking chaise lounge, supine, legs crossed at the ankles, her sunglasses held aside and squinting toward my face, which had the sun behind it. She was an absolute knockout.

I remember being disturbed by the way in which the shadow of my paunch spread itself across her own flat tan belly. Jesus, I gotta get back to the gym, I thought to myself, standing over her. I unconsciously sucked my gut in as she said, "Mr. Brennan, is it, then? From the insurance company?"

"Yeah, that's right, Mrs. Capella. Thanks for seeing me. I'm really sorry about the...situation. My condolences."

"Well, thank you. It's been a tough time for me."

"I can imagine."

It was difficult at this point to keep my eyes politely off of her truly splendid figure, blatantly displayed as it was, but between discreet glances in her direction I managed to take in the rest of the scenery, which is equally splendid in its own way.

The grounds are lavishly planted with the usual assortment of tropical flora, bougainvillea, birds-of-paradise and et cetera, all punctuated by twin rows of Italian Cypress along the borders. A rock waterfall spills into a large spa, which in turn overflows into an oversized rectangular pool accented with marble statuary. Beyond is a sweeping view of the Pacific coast, from Newport Harbor to the north to San Diego south, including ironically enough the spot just north of Laguna Beach from which ten days ago the column of smoke from Capella's wreck would have been plainly visible on the horizon, save for the fog.

The house is in an exclusive section of Pelican Hill, a high-priced development above the bluffs in the south of Newport, which I reached by a short drive from Costa Mesa, where I live, across the metaphorical train tracks separating my little berg from it's fashionable sister, down the PCH through Corona del Mar, through a very impressive Romanesque stone portico and up an Olympian hill that climbs gracefully away from the sea, breaching at last a heavy iron gate intended to insulate Mr. and Mrs. Capella and their fancy neighbors from the barbarians.

The driveway is herringbone brick, long and wide. The front yard is expansive by Orange County standards. A turquoise Mercedes convertible sits parked in front of the garage. The vanity plates feature a stylized palm with a miniature orange sun and read DLC. Everything looks very well-tended.

The housekeeper greeted me at the door, a middle-aged Hispanic lady with a soft resignation in her smile. She escorted me to the pool area by way of a quick transit of the home, a custom piece of Tuscan architecture of completely unnecessary proportion, with lots of natural stone, rich cherry-stained woods, elaborate lighting fixtures, high ceilings, gilded staircases, and a glimpse of a vast kitchen filled with stainless and granite.

"So did you bring me a check?" she asked. She was sitting up now on the lounger and facing me. The sunglasses were back on and she regarded my standing form with a studied expression of indifference.

I said, "No, Ma'am, that's someone else's department. I'm sure someone will send you the first two and a half million as soon as the paperwork is taken care of. I'm looking into your husband's death for the company. The second payment doesn't happen until we satisfy ourselves it was really accidental."

"What do you think, somebody, like, murdered Frank?"

"I'll be honest with you, we'd like, really like it if that turned out to be the case. We'd like it a lot. No offence."

She gave me a grim, brave little smile and shook her head. "You're going to be disappointed, Mr. Brennan. Frank's death was an accident, all right."

"Most likely. On the other hand, and don't get me wrong here but let's face it. He was the kind of man who got mixed reviews from those who knew him. He had his detractors, I'm saying, am I right?"

"What he had was a serious death wish. He drove like a maniac."

"And yet he was an expert driver, or so I've been led to believe."

"An expert driver, at least to hear him tell it, but, like, hopelessly reckless. His number came up. That's all, Mr. Brennan. His number came up."

A long moment of silence while we both took a moment to contemplate the reasonableness of our respective viewpoints and I used the opportunity once again to drink in the scenery.

Then, in a smaller, self-conscious voice, she said, "I suppose you'd especially like it if I were somehow involved?"

"I'm easy."

"I just bet you are. I'm not."

The expression on her face told me we were headed in the wrong direction. She was, after all, a new widow and a beautiful young girl to boot who'd spent a lifetime I'm certain having men kiss her ass, and there wasn't a reason on God's earth for me to swim against that particular tide.

"Aw, look," I said, "I'm sorry. I'm an asshole in the morning before I've had my coffee. And truth be told, we're on the hook for the first half either way. The money goes to whoever is next in line. And no one seriously believes this is anything but a very unfortunate accident, okay? Truce?"

She managed a little half-smile and reached to take my extended hand. She said, "Okay, then. Let's go inside and I'll get you some. Coffee, I mean. I'm very interested to see if that will magically transform you into someone who is not an asshole."

Ouch. But she said it with a smile and a wink.

"Believe me," I lied, "the thought that you had anything to do with your husband's death never entered my mind. I'm just crossing the T's and dotting the I's."

She led me into the house, where we took seats at the bar in what is almost certainly the largest kitchen I've ever seen, larger surely than my own entire condo, and I'm sipping a very good cup of coffee, a cappuccino that Lourdes, the housekeeper, brewed for me in a fancy piece of Swiss machinery that would make your average barista swoon with jealousy. Delilah is drinking some vile combination of fruits, vegetables, almond milk and God knows what else she whipped up in the Vitamix. Somewhere along the line she found a wrap that covered the upper part of her body, but her legs were still available in their entirety for my viewing pleasure. Her toes were splayed against the lower rung of her barstool and were painted a lovely shade of pink.

"So," she said, "I'm curious, Mr. Brennan. Like, what exactly do you want from me?"

"Call me Pat, Mrs. Capella."

"Fine. I'm Delilah. But everyone just calls me Del."

"Del, then. Thanks. Really routine. You don't have to answer any of my questions. Legally, you don't have to talk to me at all. But it would sure help, and most of what I need to know I'll find out one way or the other anyway."

"Like what?"

"Like the arrangement of your husband's financial affairs, for example. You would be the sole beneficiary of his estate, would you?"

"I'm not in Frank's will, if that's what you mean."

"Really? That's odd."

"I wasn't his first wife, okay?"

"You don't say."

"I don't know that the situation calls for sarcasm, Pat."

"You're right. Apologies. So who gets the estate?"

"He has, or had, two grown children. Frank had been divorced from his first wife for five years when met, not that that little fact has kept some in the media from suggesting I was a homewrecker. His daughter and son were preteens when the divorce occurred, and I think they still harbored hopes that their parents would reconcile. A natural thing, I guess, but trust me that was never going to happen. So anyway, they both disliked me from the start and never accepted me as their dad's wife.

"Partly to placate them, or so he said, Frank asked me to sign a prenuptial agreement. I had no problem with that. Money's nice, don't get me wrong, but I grew up living simply and my life will never revolve around money. I would never marry a man for his wealth. I loved Frank, and that's why I married him."

I said, "All right. So tell me about the prenup."

"Deal was, I was to get nothing except a very generous allowance until and unless we were still married after five years. Then I was to receive a million dollars. We were only seven months away from our fifth anniversary, by the way, so I can save you asking that question. After ten years, I would have been entitled to a full share. Until then, the kids get it all."

"The house?"

"Yes. They're selling it. They've told me I can live here for three months, and then it's going on the market."

"Well, that's a damn shame. It's a beautiful place."

"Isn't it?"

"So you're telling me the insurance is all there is for you?"

"Yes, that's right. He agreed to that to protect me in case I turned out to be a faithful wife but he died before ten years were up."

"Some would say his dying in a car accident worked out pretty well for you, then, if you don't mind my saying."

"Goddamn you, I do mind. I loved my husband, Mr. Brennan."

She spun on her bar stool and shot me a look that was equal parts anger and sadness. At that moment, looking into those baby blues of hers, I became persuaded she was probably telling the truth. She maybe really did love the guy.

"Del, I meant no offense. I'm just giving voice to the thoughts that are gonna be out there, you know?"

"You think I'm not used to that shit by now? You think that ever since the day I married Frank half this town hasn't been talking behind my back? Calling me a gold digging little whore? Waiting for me to fall on my face. Oh yeah, I'm, like, I've totally had the course."

"His friends' wives a little hard on you?"

"Sure. No woman likes competition half her age. Believe it or not, though, his buddies were worse. They treated me like a real bimbo."

"Which didn't keep them from hitting on you, I'm guessing."

"As a matter of fact, you're right. You're a real student of human nature, aren't you? They were plenty jealous of Frank, having such a pretty young wife. Meanwhile, they're all banging their secretaries themselves, every chance they get, aren't they? Newport's a tough town, Pat, for a girl from the Midwest. Sinners and hypocrites."

"Not to mention Philistines. Where'd you grow up?"

"Iowa. My Dad was a minister, which explains the name, by the way, and thanks for not asking. You're the first."

12

"You're very welcome. So how'd you meet your husband?"

"He was teaching a class I was in, believe it or not. Business law, at Orange Coast College. I came to California to go to school, and maybe get into modeling or acting. He was volunteering at the college. And thanks one more time for not making any jokes about daycare or grammar school. I've heard them all."

"My pleasure. She was sort of a dangerous girl, wasn't she?"

"Hmm?"

"Your namesake."

"Only if your name was, like, Samson."

"Hah. Right. So tell me about your husband. What did he get up to that made him so unpopular?"

"Frank grew up in Brooklyn, Mr. Brennan. He was a vicious competitor. He was about winning, and he was willing to use any tactic, no matter how underhanded, to win. You went up against him in court, you were going to come away bloodied. You and your attorney both, humiliated and embarrassed."

"Doesn't sound that groundbreaking to me."

"Trust me it was. There's a certain level of civility expected within the legal community, believe it or not."

"Okay."

"So Frank's practice was unique. He only represented wives, and then only wives who were divorcing wealthy, prominent men. Two, three cases a year, no more. Sometimes, more often than not actually, the husbands had been unfaithful. Sometimes these women were just tired of the old man. Either way the poor guys were not coming away with their portfolios or reputations intact. It was pretty brutal. 'Delilah', he used to say to me, 'I'm gonna grab that cheating bastard by the balls and squeeze until he comes to Jesus.' And he meant every word."

"I see."

"And then there was the other thing. The rumor mill claimed that after screwing the husband he'd be more than happy to do the wife, if, you know, she was feeling lonely and vulnerable and unloved like women in that position often do. The Courthouse Casanova they called him in the gossip columns."

"Salt in the wounds, huh? Were the rumors true?"

"I don't honestly know. I'm not the type to have my husband followed around. He swore they weren't and I chose to believe him. I think he enjoyed the reputation, though, either way."

"Fair to say it was a source of tension in the marriage, nonetheless?"

"Fair to say it didn't help. But it wasn't enough to make me kill him or have him killed, if that's what you're getting at."

"Not in the slightest. Sorry, just trying to fill out the whole picture, you know?"

There was a long moment, then, of silence between us. I'd tipped right up to the edge of really pissing her off, which I very much wanted to avoid doing. We needed an intermission before the next round.

After a while I said, "Well, judging by this little crib here the guy did okay for himself, money-wise. All from family law, imagine. And here I thought that was more or less the bottom of the food chain for legal practitioners."

"Hmm. Except perhaps for criminal law."

"I guess you have me there. But at least those guys' clients have it coming."

After dispensing that little gem of wisdom I glanced at her and saw that her mood had darkened. She wasn't crying, but her eyes were moist and I could see genuine pain in them.

"Everybody in this town has it coming, Pat, believe me. Everybody has it coming." And then, "Frank, he had a hard shell. But he had a softer side, as well, the side I fell in love with."

I said, "Look, I'm gonna tell you what it is, okay? Insurance executives are a very paranoid lot, and not completely without reason. Everybody is trying to scam them. It's the real national pastime. Mostly we're talking small time insurance fraud, slip and fall and that sort of nonsense. But sometimes something bigger, like maybe murdering a spouse to collect the life insurance. Bearing that in mind, I can tell you there are things they don't like about your husband's accident. And to be fair, in anybody's book including mine there is indeed much not to like about your husband's accident. Like, he was a very well regarded race-trained driver. Like, he managed to slide his car through the one small spot in the county where the highway railing was down. Like, the age difference in this marriage and his fat insurance policy. Et cetera.

"Now as I see it you would have to be a goddamn genius to have pulled this off yourself. I don't see any way. I lean toward it's a case of over exuberance on the part of your husband coupled with exceptionally bad luck.

"But what the hell, I'm getting $500 a day plus an unlimited expense account to chase my tail around on this thing, so for a little while I get to eat steak and drink wine instead of hamburger and beer. Plus I don't have to spend my evenings parked outside some sleazy hotel spying on even sleazier middle-aged adulterers.

"Anyway, Mrs. Capella, I wouldn't lose any sleep over it. I'm sure there's nothing there. I'll let myself out."

Looking back at it now, I realize that I had made my mind up five minutes in that she had nothing to do with her husband's death. She simply oozed innocence and sincerity. She had me mostly convinced she loved her husband, and I was going to have to find another suspect, a long shot at this point, or accept that Capella's death was accidental.

I was of two minds, driving away from the Casa Capella and the ether wearing off a little. On the one hand, if I was going to make any serious money out of this deal I needed to prove somebody whacked Delilah's husband. So who benefits? Delilah was the number one logical choice, as good a possibility as any, and clearly the one person who gained the most from his premature demise.

On the other hand, sending a precious creature like her to prison would be an unspeakable waste, and so I was relieved despite everything to find I had great difficulty believing her capable of murder.

CHAPTER 5

ARCHIE FENNER

"It was like the whole thing happened in slow motion. I can still see it, like watching a movie in my head. She came off right up there, you can see there's a gap in the railing, and of course the burn marks. It was real foggy that morning, and it was as if the car just materialized, flying through space. I couldn't believe my eyes. It was spinning flat, real slow like, and then it bounced off the hillside and started to tumble end over end, until it impacted tail first on that group of boulders you see over there."

Archie Fenner raised a slender, sunburned arm and pointed for my benefit to a pile of large rocks blackened by the explosion and still covered with small pieces of charred Porsche debris, with a nasty-looking black plume of scorched earth rising on the bluff wall nearly to road level. A couple of clumps of prickly pear cactus, the odd stand of pampas grass and a yucca or two had been clinging to the side of the hill but were torched in its wake. The main body of wreckage had been lifted out two days earlier by crane.

Archie was the only living soul, as far as we know, to have witnessed Frank Capella's spectacular death dive. He lived in one of a small number of mobile homes still left in the cove at the bottom, a little village that time and the developers forgot.

"You know what it was like?" he said to me. "It was like watching the Challenger blow up that awful day, all so slow and unthinkable and… surreal. Like it couldn't really be happening, what your eyes are telling you. Of course, Challenger was a part of me, so it was much worse. That was a bad day. Helped build her, you know."

"You're kidding. You worked on the space shuttle?"

"Sure did. That and a lot of earlier space programs. Retired as an engineer for Rockwell ten years ago, and Martha and I moved down here."

"Here" was described by a distracted sweep of the arm.

We stood on a crescent of sand perhaps a hundred yards wide at low tide, tucked into a rocky cove at the north end of Laguna Beach, a hundred feet below the Pacific Coast Highway, on which traffic is beginning to pick up as the morning lengthens. Behind us the sea was gray in the flat early light, the morning overcast was still hiding the sun, and the gulls were standing around on the sand like they were waiting for something to happen. Down the beach a ways a man was surfcasting. A quarter-mile to the north a college-age girl in running shorts and an iPod strapped to her forearm was coming our way, padding along the hard-packed sand just above the waterline. Out on the ocean a pair of surfers in black wetsuits worked the low breakers.

Archie was a man in his seventies, medium height with salt and pepper hair spraying out from beneath a faded baseball cap, skin age-mottled and deeply tanned, to the point that he almost matched the reddish-brown of his golden retriever, tagging faithfully along behind us. He wore a T-shirt that looked to have made maybe a couple dozen too many trips through the wash cycle, a pair of threadbare dungarees and flip-flops. But a bright light burned in his eyes, and though scrawny he was well-muscled and looked like if you gave him a little notice he could up and run a marathon for you. He was an engineer, I was relieved to learn, a man therefore intelligent and unexcitable and a reliable witness.

I said, "Okay, Mr. Fenner, I appreciate your taking the time to speak with me. Tell me everything you can remember about that day. If you would, just start at the beginning."

"Sure. Not really a lot to tell. I came out of the trailer around six o'clock. It was a Sunday morning. Figured I'd do some fishing until Martha got up and made my breakfast. She likes to sleep in."

"Your wife?"

"Right. So it was a cold and foggy morning, nothing moving on the highway, I was standing down there, near the water line, with my pole stuck in the sand and just sort of enjoying the peace, you know, when I started to hear this engine noise, really wound up, lots of shifting, somebody really wringing his car out and I thought to myself what kind of maniac would drive like that in this fog? Mind you, the heavy air suppresses

17

the sound, so it was coming through muffled and I thought it was coming from farther away than it was. Then suddenly I realized it was almost on top of me, which is when I turned around to look up at the roadway, to see if I could get a glimpse of the car as it went by. Then a funny thing happened…the engine just quit."

"Quit? You mean he backed off the throttle?"

"More like it cut out. I mean I heard nothing but the tires squealing a little. Must've been two, three seconds. Then she comes flying through the air, big as hell, ass end first and I'm just standing here dumbfounded. About the time the car becomes airborne the engine cuts back in, the throttle opens up wide and of course with the wheels spinning free the engine just winds right up to red line, which is what it was doing at impact. Christ, what an explosion. Thing must have been absolutely full of gas. He never had a chance, the poor son-of-a-bitch."

"And so, but, he must have hit the brakes before he lost control. Did you hear him braking?"

"Not in the slightest. Look for yourself. There are no skid marks. It was like he lost it so fast he didn't even realize it until he looks out the window and sees he's an airplane pilot."

CHAPTER 6

BRAD JOHNSON

The OC Weekly is one of those tabloid throwaways you find in most big cities these days, modeled on the winning formula originally pioneered by the Village Voice in NYC. Up front you have your warmed over sixties-era left-wing politics and socially enlightened reportage on the civic minutiae of Orange County. The middle section features reviews of completely unwatchable foreign movies and various local untalented garage bands, plus ads from a collection of charlatans operating under the rubric of alternative medicine. And the back third, where the bills get paid: a sex market masquerading as a classified section and posting not totally unentertaining advertisements from hookers, strip clubs and assorted amateur freaks and perverts.

Alternative press, they like to call it, but this is not a periodical you read for breaking news, unless it's news to you that America is going to hell and the capitalists are driving.

Except that when I pulled into the car wash on my way home from Archie's and settled in for a little light reading while waiting, I found that the Weekly had stumbled onto a real scoop in the Brad Johnson case. Somebody at the paper had secured his little black book, and they were having a ball exposing the distinguished list of his friends and accomplices.

Brad Johnson, popularly known as "Longboard," had been an enduring fixture of the Huntington Beach scene for the last couple of decades. He was a certified piece of work, teen surf champ turned middle-aged surf bum and man-about-town, one of those guys who are famous for being famous. He was good-looking, late thirties, tall, lean, tanned and blonde, always the life of the party and always surrounded by girls.

Nobody was ever really sure what he did for a living. Maybe he sold a little dope, maybe he kept a couple of well-heeled older ladies company, nothing too taxing or too legitimate. And of course he surfed, daily.

However, Mr. Brad had recently gotten his ass into a real wringer with the authorities. Seems that even though he could get most girls, he couldn't have them all and it was the ones who said no that really tickled his fancy, which dilemma he had taken to solving with the help of a little GHB in the water. That would be Gamma Hydroxybutyrate, the so-called date rape drug. One of his victims had tumbled to the situation, having awakened naked and used in his bed one weekend morning, and subsequently filed a complaint. The ensuing search of his residence turned up any number of lurid and highly incriminating videos of sessions he had taped with a series of drugged-out young girls, some of whom he'd unfortunately neglected to card.

Now this situation was attended with an enormous amount of excitement along the OC coast. Everybody was having terrific fun with it, as Brad's contacts were far-flung and distributed along every rung of the class ladder. But for me the situation held very little interest. Personally, I couldn't care less what Longboard got up to in his free time; I have my own problems. But I had a sudden change of heart when I happened to glance near the end of the article the name, among those in his book, of one Delilah Capella, widow of the prominent and recently deceased attorney Francis Capella. What the hell was she doing hanging with this creep? I would have to file this one away for future consideration.

When I left the car wash that afternoon I drove back to my condo in Costa Mesa, sat around for a while watching nothing particular on television, and eventually decided to make myself dinner. Grilled a steak out on the deck, popped a Corona, put my feet up on the rail, and just started thinking about stuff in general.

Winter in Southern California is absolutely my favorite season. The air is crisp and clean in a way that clears your mind, which is what I needed. Two things were bothering me. First, about the engine on Capella's Porsche cutting out. I felt strongly that Archie was to be trusted on that point, but it just didn't make any sense. I could see the guy getting into a turn too deep and too fast, and having to back off a little on the power. But even I know that in a situation like that to just totally lift off the throttle is a chump move, disastrously destabilizing, and Capella was no chump when it came to driving. So where did that leave us? Engine failure? What were the odds of that? Zero, close enough.

And then there was the Del and Brad thing. What the hell was up with that? She had me convinced she's just a sweet, innocent small town girl, and suddenly it turns out she's connected to the sex, drugs and surf crowd up in Huntington Beach. Was I getting played for a sucker, or was she going to be able to give me a legitimate explanation for that happy piece of news? We really needed to have another chat.

CHAPTER 7

DELILAH

I had come once again to the Capella home, and I lay uneasily beside his widow. She was for the moment displeased. Very displeased. She was sprawled on the chaise lounge next to me, prone this time, legs spread slightly and her rump perched petulantly in the air. She was wearing what I am beginning to assume is her standard uniform of the day, a microscopic little string bikini. Despite her mood she was a genuine delectation, pardon the pun.

After a few moments of ominous silence I opened my eyes and sat up to gaze at the ocean. It had rained again the day before and the sky was scrubbed as clean and transparent as glass. To the south San Clemente Island lay stretched along the horizon. A couple of pelicans cruised along the coastline. The white sails of a dozen small boats were like so much litter on the blue water.

Del had a habit of falling silent for a while after any conversation that might be construed in the slightest to be confrontational, I was learning. Not a pout, exactly, but more a helpful pause, an opportunity for me to reflect on my unreasonableness. Thus have the last ten minutes passed, she rolled over on her belly, head on folded arms, eyes closed, and me, in street clothes, shifting awkwardly between lying on a chaise I pulled beside her and staring into the sky, or sitting up and staring at the sea.

I asked her, of course, about Longboard. It was the ostensible reason for my visit, after all, though to be honest the thought of simply seeing her again was as much my motivation as any.

"It's really no big deal, Mr. Brennan. I met him once, a couple times maybe, years ago. He was a collector…he kept every phone number he ever came across."

"How's about you call me Pat, like before, and I'll call you, Del, Mrs. Capella, are you good with that? And I need at this point for you to be absolutely up front and honest with me, okay?"

"I am, Pat. When I first moved to Southern California I lived with a roommate in Huntington Beach. I needed a place to stay, and I found this situation in the want ads. Her name was Angie, and she was sort of a free spirit, and she introduced me to Brad. He seemed all right at first, but I eventually began to realize that he was like, big into drugs, as was Angie, and lots of wild partying, and at that time the whole town of Huntington Beach it seemed was all about surfing and screwing and getting high. Not my scene. Very shortly thereafter I found my own place in Westminster, and moved out. But Brad never threw away a page from his black book, I guess."

"And that's the extent of it? I'm not going to find out later there was more? Like maybe you were scoring from him?"

That's when she got angry. She had thrown on a wrap when first I showed up, to my great disappointment, and had to this point remained covered up with it. But now she stood and threw it onto the pool deck. She picked up her drink from the ground, a very unappetizing green concoction of pressed vegetable juices that Lourdes had blended up for her, and waved it in my face.

"Look at me. Do I look like someone who doesn't spend a whole lot of time taking care of herself? Like somebody who sits around getting high? You think I'm drinking this shit for any reason other than my health, Mr. Brennan?"

She had me there. "Hey, look, Del…now you have me feeling like an asshole again. Sorry, but I'm just doing my job. Obviously you are not a regular user of illegal substances. Very obviously you keep yourself in splendid shape. Doesn't mean you couldn't be doing a line here or there. I had to ask."

As I spoke I was sitting straight up on the chaise. She placed herself directly in front of me, bent over, grabbed a handful of her waist-length hair and slapped it against my face.

"So here you go," she said. "Here's about a year's worth of record. Help yourself…run tests if you want."

At which point she flopped onto her lounger and fell into silence.

I stood up and prepared to leave. "So I'll be letting myself out. Sorry if I offended you, Del, I really am. I have neither the legal authority nor the inclination to test you for drugs. I just had to ask, is all."

No answer.

"Anyway, this isn't about drugs. It's about a dead lawyer. I should be filing my report soon, and I imagine you'll see your check shortly thereafter So maybe we'll talk again, another time?"

"Maybe."

That's where it could have lain, and perhaps should have lain, come to think of it. Delilah was a sweet young girl who in no way, shape or form was capable of killing anybody. I was maybe falling for her, but any thoughts of a connection with her were in the realm of pure fantasy. She was too young, too good-looking and probably too rich for me. She was out of my league and there was no way I could ever have her, so why keep pressing my nose to the glass?

I had, in sum, no case and no girl.

Frank, on the other hand, was the lucky guy who had her, had everything, in fact, including the world by the balls. Dumb ass threw it all away in one reckless moment, and that was that, end of story.

* * *

Except that as I left the house I made a random decision that ended up changing everything. For no really good reason other than morbid curiosity I decided to go take a look at the spot where Capella left the road and to view the accident scene from the top down.

Once I hit the Pacific Coast Highway I turned left, toward Laguna Beach. The twisting road took me through one of the last unspoiled pieces of coastline between here and the Mexican border, Crystal Cove State Park, a broad swath of chaparral and grassland along a bluff between Newport and Laguna. Approaching the north end of town I passed the turnoff for the narrow road leading down to Archie's trailer park. I slowed and found the accident site, a tight outside turn a couple hundred yards farther down the highway. A shiny new section of guardrail was in place, but from my car I saw no further evidence of the crash. I had to continue south for maybe another quarter mile before I could find a safe spot to pull off and park.

A couple of minutes of walking brought me back to where Capella's car launched itself into space. I stood with my knees braced against the new railing. Just beyond was the fresh scar where the top of the bluff had given way, the collapse leaving a wedge scooped from the hillside with an ugly mound of dirt, old railing and uprooted plant material humped up at the bottom. Past that another twenty yards or so down the hillside was the site of the initial impact, and from there an ugly path of scorched rock and acacia led to the Porsche's final resting place on the beach, a good hundred feet down. They'd done a good job of cleaning up, though. I searched in vain for any sign of automobile parts. To the casual observer it looked as if a bunch of local teenagers might have built a bonfire that got out of control.

The view from where I stood was a gorgeous one, and I took a few minutes to enjoy it. The cold front carrying our most recent rains had passed on through, leaving the air smelling of salt and wet mesquite. It was still quite cool and the wind on my face was fresh and bracing. To the southeast, down toward the Mexican border, a thin layer of cirrus clouds rode high in the sky, and to the west a much lower layer of stratocumulus was sliding slowly my way. The buildups were white and unthreatening. Occasionally one floated in front of the sun, casting a long black shadow onto the wind-swept water. Something in the way of a new storm was brewing in the Pacific hundreds of miles to the south, off the Baja coast, and the waves were already beginning to build. There was a good-sized crowd of surfers enjoying the ride.

Below me were the huddled trailers of Archie's community, each with a white picket fence and colored marine flags flying, each with a miniature garden of potted ornamental plants, each with a wooden boardwalk leading through the sea grass to the flat wet sand.

To my left was a headland that extended away from the highway and rose another fifty feet or so above me. There was some expensive real estate built on top of it and I could just catch a glimpse of tiled roofline through the trees. I noticed what appeared to be a trail leading across its near face. It was worn into the hillside at road level, so that on one side the terrain rose away, while on the other it descended toward the beach. I decided to take a walk and see how far around I could get.

It was narrow and overgrown with manzanita, acacia and other native vegetation that afforded privacy and shelter from the ocean breeze. On the uphill side there were several spots where low, flat-topped boulders made for natural seating. I could imagine young lovers using them as romantic hideaways, availing themselves of the splendid sunset views. One of the groups of rocks afforded a good look at the oncoming southbound traffic, and it looked as if more than one person had spent some time there. Several beer cans and a liquor bottle were scattered in the hollow, along with about a pack's worth of cigarette butts.

The trail petered out just as it was beginning to curve around to the beach side. By now the sun was getting low in the sky and I turned to leave. As I got about halfway back there was a break in the clouds. A shaft of light hit the hillside below me, and glinted off of something metallic. I scrambled down, holding onto whatever branches I could find, until I came to the stand of pampas grass where I'd seen the flash. I pulled a glove out of my jacket pocket, fished around for a few minutes and pulled out a stainless steel coffee thermos. It was creased and half-covered with soot, but otherwise it was intact and I could hear liquid sloshing when I shook it. It was engraved with the monogram FAC.

My, my. So Mai's boys weren't as thorough as I'd given them credit for. When I returned to the spot with the smoked cigarettes I grabbed a handful and wrapped them in a handkerchief to take with me. I'm not sure why, but something was bothering me about them. Only later did I realize what it was: they were all the same brand.

When I got back to my car I placed the cigarette butts in one Ziploc bag, the thermos in another, larger bag, threw them both in my trunk, and pulled out my phone to call Mai.

CHAPTER 8
MINGEE

The next morning I sat across from Mai in a noisy little Mexican café in downtown Santa Ana. We were each eating breakfast burritos and drinking black coffee. Two blocks away was the Orange County Civic Center, which includes courthouses, various Federal, state and county offices, and, most relevantly, OC Sheriff's Headquarters.

Mai was displeased with me, and I was being reprimanded. On the floor next to her sat a paper bag, within which was the Ziploc containing Capella's coffee mug.

"Pat," she said, "Does the phrase 'chain of custody' ring any bells for you?"

She was unhappy that I had brought her the thermos, rather than calling and having sheriff personnel pick it up.

"Since when has your department been so fastidious about handling evidence, Mingee? Did that Register exposé I read about the way you guys operate get it wrong? Planted evidence, tampered witnesses, jailhouse beatings and such?"

"Very funny, Pat. Look, you know as well as I do that even in the very unlikely event there's any value to this particular piece of evidence, it can now never be used in court. So what am I supposed to do?"

I said, "Lie, of course. I mean, come on Mingee. A, this is just a coffee mug. It means nothing. I just wanted to complete your collection of Capella debris for you. B, I *am* a licensed investigator, which makes me almost an officer of the court. I treated it with great care. I picked it up with gloved hand and placed it immediately in the bag you see. I didn't compromise it in any way. C, how long have you known me? You telling me I can't be trusted? And number four, I'm just trying to save your CSI people from being embarrassed. Face it, baby…they're much better in Miami."

She laughed and shook her head. "You watch too much TV, is your problem."

"You know *your* problem, Mingee?"

"No, Pat, I actually don't. That's one reason I was so looking forward to seeing you this morning. I was anxious to receive the benefit of your wisdom. Please, enlighten me."

"You strive for excellence in a world of mediocrity, my beautiful little friend. By the book just doesn't get it on this particular planet. You want to play by the rules? Are you out of your mind? You think anybody in DC or Wall Street is playing by any rules? You're an immigrant, I get that, it's always been about measuring up for you. But you're swimming against the tide.

"Trust me, nobody but you gives a damn about chain of custody or any other legal nicety as long as the bad guys get caught. I know in this case it makes no difference, it's an insignificant piece of evidence, but I'm making a general point here."

We both lapsed into silence at this point, and went to work on the burritos. I motioned the waitress over to refill my coffee cup. Mai spent a few moments staring out the window.

Then she said, out of the blue, "Remember you were asking about toxicology the other day, Pat? That's unfortunately not going to be possible. I spoke with Massey over at the coroner's office. Nothing left of the body that hasn't been completely carbonized. He says you take your average Egyptian mummy, you dip him in tar and roll him in burnt toaster shakings, and you get a picture of what Capella looks like at the moment. One very crispy critter.

"However, it turns out our team found a thermos that belonged to Mr. Capella. Must have been thrown from the car as it exploded. Landed in a clump of pampas grass. It took a very thorough search to turn it up. Anyway, there was still coffee in it, so we're going to be able to do a workup on it. That should answer your question as to whether he may have been drinking before the accident. Who knows, maybe it's Irish coffee. We'll see."

I suppressed a smile. "You don't say? Well I'm sure it'll come back clean, but it will tie up a loose end, so that's good. Congratulate your people for me, that's very good work."

CHAPTER 9
PROFESSOR TREVOR SCOTT, PHD

Frank Capella's death gave every appearance of having been completely accidental, so I was pretty much just spinning my wheels at this point. I had nothing better to do, though, so I decided I'd drive down to my alma mater, UC Irvine, and talk to my old friend, Professor Scott. Doc taught a freshman physics course I took, back in the day. We hit it off and we've stayed in touch. We share a passion for automobiles that neither of us can afford. As it happens, he's an acknowledged expert in vehicle dynamics and an occasional contributor to Road and Track magazine, which is published in Newport. I figured he would be the guy to talk to for insight into the crash. I gave him a call and set a meeting for the next morning.

Doctor Scott's office looks just about like you'd figure a professor of physics office would look like, which is to say completely shambolic. Books and papers are stacked everywhere in random piles. Computer gear and assorted clutter bury his desk. The wall behind him is covered floor to ceiling with bookshelves. Hung on the wall to my left is a large chalkboard filled with mathematical hieroglyphics, and to my right hang framed poster blow-ups of the physics pantheon: Newton, Einstein, Bohr and Hawking.

The room is small, and when Trevor stood to greet me his size made it look smaller still. He is a very large man, and you'd think NFL lineman rather than professor if not for the thick wire-rimmed glasses. He's bald but has graying salt and pepper muttonchops and beard. He'd just come from the racquetball court to meet me, and he was wearing a sweatshirt, gym shorts and track shoes. There was still a sheen of perspiration on his skin, which is the color of weathered copper.

"Hey, Doc." I said "Good morning. Thanks for seeing me."

"My pleasure, Patrick. Had to come in anyway to grade some tests. What's up?"

"You heard about the Capella accident, right?"

"Yes, sure, I heard. Broke my heart. My whole life I've wanted a Carrera, as you well know."

"Yeah, I hear you. The world will get along fine with one less lawyer, but what a tragic waste to lose a Porsche. So tell me, professor. How does a guy with his experience manage to drive himself off a cliff in good weather and on dry pavement? I have an insurance company as a client that would love to know the answer to that particular question."

"Well, the roadway was dry, true, but as far as the weather being good… it was very foggy I understand, and visibility was limited. That almost certainly played a role in the accident. Anyway, it was a classic case of trailing throttle oversteer, would be my guess. Porsches are famous for it. Or I should say notorious, perhaps."

"Okay, oversteer. I've heard the term, but I'm not sure I understand it completely."

He moved over to the blackboard behind his desk, cleared a swath through the math equations with an eraser and picked up a nub of chalk.

"Let's consider," he said, "an automobile traveling through a turn. What happens as the speed increases or the radius of the turn decreases, so that the limits of tire adhesion are approached?"

He illustrated the situation with a crude drawing.

I said, "One of three things, I guess. The car slows down, the turn is shallowed out, or the car goes off the road."

"Right. Very good, Patrick. So let's consider the case where the speed is increased until in fact the car departs the pavement. Which end lets loose first, front or rear? That can be a complicated discussion. Assuming an absolutely uniform distribution of mass and a constant velocity, either end is equally likely to swing out, or both let go simultaneously.

"Of course, no real car is built like that. Most passenger cars are front heavy and, like a pendulum, are going to want to plow off the road front first. This tendency is called understeer, because the car wants to go straight rather than follow the turn the driver is steering. For your ordinary driver this is generally considered desirable for one simple reason. Say John Q or Mrs. Q are out in the family sedan and get carried away and find themselves in a situation where they're in a turn and realize they're going too fast and what do they do?"

"Back off the throttle."

"Exactly, or even brake hard, God help them. Now here's the thing. When this happens, the weight of the vehicle shifts forward on its suspension, putting more weight on the front wheels, giving them more traction. Luckily for them, that's the pair of wheels that really need it. The car stays on the road long enough to slow to a safe speed. It's all good."

"I see. Makes sense."

"Yes it does, and that's the way Detroit builds automobiles. But now let's look at the case of a rear engine car like the Porsche Carrera. It's a vehicle that oversteers. Because that's where the mass is, the rear end wants to swing out, which would have the effect of tightening the turn. That means the rear tires are doing most of the work pulling the car through the turn, and they are going to want to let go first. What happens now if the driver lifts, or 'trails' the throttle?"

I said, "I see your point. Weight shifts forward, decreasing the traction of the tires in back. Bad news."

"Correct. A plus, Patrick. Very bad news, indeed, and believe me many a novice Porsche driver has come to serious grief learning the news the hard way.

"The engineers in Zuffenhausen have worked over the years to improve the situation with every kind of tricky suspension setup, and they're better, the newer models. But they can still bite you.

"Now interestingly enough, in the hands of a skilled race driver, this effect can actually be very useful, which is why Porsches are so popular on the amateur circuits, especially with slalom type races."

"How's that?"

"If you know what you're doing you can use oversteer to your advantage, to get around a turn faster. You induce the oversteer to get the rear end starting to hang out, get the nose around, and then get back on the throttle to catch it. In other words, you modulate the effect and make it work for you. It's tricky, it gets some getting used to, but it can be mastered."

"And so, but, Capella would have been skilled at this, right? He did a lot of amateur racing and had a reputation as being pretty good."

"Doesn't mean you can't make a mistake, Patrick. Even Michael Jordan missed a game winner now and then. Tiger Woods occasionally bogies a hole or two. Remember what I taught you in Physics 101? That chapter on quantum mechanics you enjoyed so much? Anything that can happen will, eventually."

"Sounds like a sophisticated version of Murphy's Law to me, Doc."

"Now that you mention it."

"Okay. So let's just say I'm willing to dismiss the amazing coincidence that this happens at exactly the spot where the guardrail is down. Let's talk about the engine cutting out. The witness said it quit completely for a few seconds. Any thoughts on that?"

"Sure. The witness is wrong, I'm certain. It dropped to idle, and in comparison to the noise it was making before it seemed to him that it stopped. It didn't, it just got very much quieter than it had been. You said yourself it was foggy that morning down on the beach. Heavy, wet air dampens sound. So Mr. Capella's out having a little romp on the public highways and byways. He's feeling frisky and he's wringing out his new car. But in the limited visibility he misjudges distances and a turn sneaks up on him faster than he expects. He reacts reflexively and loses control. Happens all the time, I'm afraid. Ask the CHP."

"Allowing him to shoot the narrow gap conveniently waiting for him, just like a Wayne Gretsky slapshot with eyes?"

"Probably not as big a coincidence as you seem to think, Patrick. Think about it. Where do they put guardrails up in the first place? Along sharp turns in the road. Where do cars go out of control most often? Along sharp turns in the road. Besides, what's your alternative explanation? You think maybe Wile E. Coyote left an oil slick for him?"

CHAPTER 10

TOXICOLOGY

Mai called me early the next morning. The first thing out of her mouth was, "Patrick, are you sitting down?"

I could hear an undertone of excitement in her voice. As it happened, I *was* sitting down, on the edge of the bed, where I'd been lying staring at the ceiling when the phone rang. I said, "As a matter of fact I am, my sweet. What's up?"

"You remember that thermos we found at the Capella accident site?"

"Uh, let me think. Yeah, sure. What of it?"

"Yes, well, the toxicology report came back a couple days ago. I just heard about the results."

I said, "Let me guess. Our pal Frank had a couple of shots in his morning coffee, right?"

"No, not actually, Patrick. As a matter of fact they found traces of GHB in it. Somebody spiked his coffee."

"You have got to be kidding. That's ridiculous. Are they sure?"

"Oh they're sure all right, at least they say they are. This is privileged information, by the way. I'm not even supposed to know."

"So how do you?"

"A friend of mine on the force has a mole in the PA's office."

"Oh really. Would that be the dope you're sleeping with?"

She gave me a big sigh and said, "That's the Patrick I know and love. Always the charmer. Yes, it's my boyfriend who told me."

"And this mole of his, with the PA, would that be some lady he's cheating on you with?"

"Goddamn it, Patrick, you are so effing adolescent. Don't pull that jealous jilted lover bullshit on me. You had your chance. All I wanted was a ring on my finger and I would never have left you. I'm trying to do you a favor here, but I'm gonna hang up if you don't cut it out."

She was right of course. We'd had this conversation more than once. She wanted marriage. I couldn't pull the trigger. I wondered briefly if it was too late but what the hell, she was probably better off with her cop, and I had other fish to fry at the moment.

I said, "Yeah, yeah, I'm sorry, you're right. Just trying to be funny. I apologize. So what are they thinking?"

"What do you think they're thinking? They're thinking what anybody would be thinking. There were two people in that house. So either Capella committed suicide in a very unconventional manner, or the little woman did him in. I can assure you that Tanaka is absolutely salivating."

"What about the housekeeper?" I asked.

Mai said, "It was Sunday morning. She has Sundays off."

"Hmm. Well I have to tell you that puzzles me more than a little. I mean, why would Delilah kill her husband?"

"Delilah? My aren't we cozy? And are you kidding? You know as well as I do that with spouses establishing motive is never an issue. Anyway, I'm pretty sure they can come up with about five million reasons 'Delilah' might want her husband gone. Accidentally, of course."

I had no response to that, and after a moment of silence Mai continued.

She said, "And then there is the very inconvenient matter of Brad Johnson's legal status. Heard about it? He is presently incarcerated and awaiting trial for using GHB on young women. The same Brad Johnson, that would be, in whose little black book the name of one Delilah Capella, nee Livingston, appears rather prominently."

"Jeez, that's right. I talked to her about that, actually, and she had a pretty innocent explanation."

"Sounds like you two have gotten real chummy, Patrick. You have eyes for her?"

"Just doing my job, Mingee."

"Uh huh. Well, I would be very careful with that, my friend. It's looking to me like your widow may have a serious legal problem. We're looking very hard into the question of whether there's a more recent link between those two. She already has a big problem, either way. But if we can connect them currently, she is well and truly screwed."

My guts were churning at this point. All I could think to say was, "Indeed."

When I hung up I made myself a cup of coffee and tried to figure out my next move. I decided that Del and I needed to have another conversation. I picked up the phone. Del didn't answer. Nor did she the rest of the day.

CHAPTER 11
DEL

The next morning I decided to drive over to the Capella residence. On the way I kept telling myself it was a professional visit, but the truth was that there was more to it than business. This girl was beginning to fascinate me.

She was home. When she opened the front door, she was white as a ghost. Her face was ashen. Absolutely drained. Blanco. I said, "My God, Delilah. What's wrong?"

"They picked me up, Patrick. Yesterday morning. Two sheriffs. They drove me downtown to Santa Ana and interrogated me for three hours. It was horrible. Nothing in my life has prepared me for an experience like that."

So that's why she didn't answer my calls. I wondered if Mai knew that was going to happen. Almost certainly she did. Apparently she didn't trust me not to warn Del, a fact I found mildly annoying.

I said, "So what did they ask you?"

"They wanted to know what Frank and I had done the day before and morning of his accident."

"What did you tell them?"

"The truth."

"Of course, but specifically."

"That day we just pretty much hung around the house. Frank was taking a break and had no active cases. Around lunch time I grilled some salmon on the barbeque and we each had a glass of wine out on the pool deck. In the midafternoon we watched a movie. We went to bed very early, I'd say around seven. Frank had just a couple weeks before traded in his old Carrera for a shiny new one and he was planning to take it out for a spin early the next day. He liked to drive down the coast to Laguna and then pick up the 133 toll road north toward Riverside. Early weekend mornings there's very little traffic and there are no patrol cars, so it's perfect for him to wring his car out, as he used to call it.

"We made love and fell asleep. I woke up at four, threw on some gym clothes and sneakers and drove his car down the hill to gas it up. Back home I brewed him two Americano coffees and poured them into his thermos. He was up and showered when I got back. We had a brief conversation, I kissed him goodbye and he drove away just about right at daybreak."

"How come you got his gas? Why didn't he just stop on the way down the coast himself?"

"Well, partly it was because the nearest gas is the other way, up the coast. Going south you're all the way to Laguna before you see a station. Plus it was our little thing, a treat for me. Frank wouldn't ordinarily let me drive his Turbo. It was too much car for me, he said, and I suppose he was right. But he would let me take it on short little trips like that."

"I see. I assume it was a manual transmission, right? You can drive a stick?"

"Amazing, isn't it? I'm not some OC princess, Pat. I grew up in a country town. I learned to drive when I was twelve, and my family never owned a vehicle with an automatic transmission."

"I see. Sorry, didn't mean to offend."

Suddenly Delilah broke out in uncontrolled fits of sobbing. She said, "They found Frank's coffee thermos, Patrick. There was some sort of drug in it. Something to make him sleepy. They think I killed him, Patrick. I just cannot believe this is happening."

I decided not mention that I knew about the GHB.

"So let's see. You personally saw to it that your husband's car was topped off with fuel, making it more likely that any accident he might have would be fatal. Then you hand his coffee thermos to him, which just happens to be spiked with a sleep-inducing drug. Beautiful, effing beautiful."

"It looks bad, doesn't it?"

"Bad? Bad doesn't begin to describe it, sweetheart."

"What am I going to do?"

"Jesus. I don't know. Get a lawyer, for sure. Stop talking to the cops, or anyone else for that matter. That's step one. Not another word until you have representation. Did they ask you to take a polygraph?"

"I offered. They declined."

"No kidding? Probably afraid you'd pass."

There followed a few moments of awkward silence, and then she said, "Aren't you going to ask me?"

"Ask you what?"

"If I did it."

"No."

"I didn't. I swear it. I loved Frank, like I told you. I told you the truth."

"I never doubted it, Delilah. The question is how the hell anything got into that thermos. I can't imagine an answer to that. But we'll find it, whatever it is. I believe you. I'm going to help you."

Del took my hand with an oddly tentative gesture and guided me into the living room, where we sat down on the couch side by side. Minutes passed in another interval of silence that under different circumstances I would have found uncomfortable.

I can't say whether it was an attraction that had already existed, or whether it was the shock and fear of her situation that created for Del the desperate need of the psychological safety and comfort of a man's physical contact. Most likely the latter, I suppose.

Whatever the reason, and without benefit of the usual preliminaries, we fell more or less spontaneously into each other's arms. It began with Delilah hugging me and holding me to her as tightly as she could, as if her life depended on not letting me go. But before I knew what was happening, and without a spoken word between us, I found myself in her bedroom, in her bed, and making love to her.

All my young life I've cut corners and pushed boundaries, but this was the most unprofessional act I had ever committed. What can I tell you? The spirit is willing but the flesh is weak.

God help me it was wonderful. It was sublime. It was transcendent. She may have been a preacher's daughter, but Del knew her way around the *boudoir*. I really had to wonder how Frank could have found it necessary to cheat on this girl.

Our lovemaking had a sort of animal urgency and emotional intensity I had never experienced before. It turns out that adrenaline is a powerful aphrodisiac.

When it was over we lay wordlessly, cuddling, for what must have been half an hour. It was I who broke the silence. I said, "Del, is it possible your housekeeper had a hand in this?"

She said, "Lourdes? She was off that morning. She didn't work weekends. It was just Frank and me."

"Is it possible she could have left something in the thermos?"

"Lourdes ran the dishwasher and unloaded it the last thing before leaving Friday. I suppose it's possible she could have put something in Frank's thermos before she left. I probably never would have noticed. But why would she possibly do that? It doesn't make sense. Nothing makes sense. It's a nightmare."

It was then the waterworks started up again, and she began to cry up a storm. I hugged her harder and wiped away her tears with the pillowcase.

She sobbed, "I need a friend, Patrick. I feel so alone right now."

"I'm here for you, Del," I said, "and I'm going to help you, I promise. I'm an investigator, remember? I'll get to the bottom of this. We just need to get it together and start thinking. We need to find a logical explanation. Your husband had a ton of enemies. Plenty of them wanted him dead, I'm sure. One figured out a way to make it happen, and to pin it on you in the bargain."

She gave me with a weak little smile and said, "Okay, thank you Pat. Thank you thank you thank you."

"You're welcome. So let's get dressed and have a drink and a brainstorming session, what do you say?"

"Okay."

Watching her put her clothes back on that slender little figure of hers, I was struck by how girlish and innocent she looked. And how vulnerable. I found it powerfully attractive. I was going to be her lover. I was going to be her lifeline.

* * *

Delilah got me a beer and blended up one of her fruit and wheat grass drinks for herself, after which we proceeded to the pool deck and lay down next to each other on chaise lounges. Neither of us spoke for a long while, though my mind was racing and I was certain hers was as well.

Finally I said, "Okay Del, let's take a look at this situation and see if we can get it sorted out."

"Okay," She answered with a whisper.

"We know that somebody somewhere along the line put GHB in your husband's coffee thermos, and we know said somebody is not you. So what possibilities does that leave us? Either it was there when he left, or he stopped somewhere, maybe to meet someone, and it was introduced at that time. One of those two scenarios has to be true, am I right?"

Del said, "Sure, yeah, I guess so."

"And so if it was there when he left, who could have put it there? One possibility is Lourdes, correct? Anyone else been at the house, any workmen, any cable guys, any delivery men or pool boys or gardeners or any, and forgive me for this but I have to know, any gentlemen callers?"

"Goddamn it, Patrick."

"Sorry, Delilah, but I have to look at every conceivable possibility. I don't know if you have quite tumbled to it yet, sweetheart, but you are in some very warm water here. If I'm to help you, I have to do what I do."

"All right, yes, I understand and appreciate it. Other than Lourdes, Frank and myself no one had been in the house for at least the week before his...accident. And for the record, just so we clear the air here, I have never been unfaithful to my husband. Let's get that straight for good."

I said, "Fair enough. We'll put that issue to bed, no pun intended."

"Thank you."

"Don't mention it. So far, then, we have Lourdes as the only person of interest with scenario number one. It also occurs to me that besides yourself she was the only person who would even have known about Frank's early morning drives, or that he took coffee along with him, right? What do you think?"

"I think that's crazy. She had absolutely no reason to harm Frank. He got along with her much better than I did. He's the one who hired her. Now she's out of a job."

"You let her go?"

"His kids did. They're calling the shots as far as the house and office go. They've wasted like no time taking over."

"I see. Well, it's not out of the question that someone got to her. We'll leave the question of who until later, for now."

We lapsed into silence again. It was another one of those late winter, early spring days in Orange County when the morning fog burns off early, the onshore breeze freshens and the sun is bright but riding low in the sky.

The view from the pool terrace is framed by twin rows of tall Italian cypress trees. The crescent of sea visible beyond is a pure and deep cerulean blue, flecked with whitecaps driven by the wind and dappled by black pools of shadow cast by the scattered cloud deck drifting eastward. The gulls and pelicans are hard at work cruising the surface of the water, their wings gently wobbling in the shifting breeze. This morning they have company, a Cessna single engine plane towing a Corona banner up and down the beach. Catalina Island is still shrouded in mist on the southwestern horizon.

Delilah noticed that my beer was finished and offered to get me another. I shook my head no. She stood, took my hand and gently kissed the back of it. She stripped off her wrap and dove into the pool, barely leaving a ripple. She proceeded to spin out a dozen or so laps. When she emerged she toweled off, drew her wrap back on, and plopped down on the chaise next to me.

I said, "So then we have scenario number two. Is it possible your husband met someone, or stopped anywhere, before the, well, you know. A business associate, maybe, or a client? Or possibly, forgive me for asking, a little Sunday morning booty call?"

Del said, "I don't think so. He never did business on weekends. Anyway, I don't think he would have had much time between leaving here and the crash happening. 'Booty' calls were never his style, by the way."

"Okay, sorry. So we're left with Lourdes."

"Seems like it. As hard as that is to believe."

"Well, let's go with that for now. And assume she would never have done it on her own. Someone must have paid her. That leaves us with figuring out who hated your husband enough to kill him."

"Hah. That's not a very exclusive club, I'm afraid. You know his reputation."

"Yes I do. So can we get access to his office files?"

"That's going to be a problem. Like I said, his kids have moved fast to take control of his estate. Frank had an office down at Newport Center.

They've closed it, grabbed all his records, and fired his secretary. They're not going to be helpful. They've never been fond of me. They took me for a gold digger from the get go and have always resented my presence in their father's life."

"Right. I remember you mentioned that the day we met."

"The good news is that Frank had very few clients. Like I told you, he represented only very high profile plaintiffs, exclusively women, and his cases were always extremely complicated and extremely lengthy. He liked to share the gory details with me, and so I can probably give you a pretty good run down if you give me time to think about it."

"Okay, tell you what. I have some research to do myself. I have a friend in the OC Sheriff's office and I'm going to try to find out what they know. I'll pull the accident report and maybe have another chat with Archie Fenner, the witness down on the beach. You rack your brains for all the information you can give me on Frank's cases, particularly of the last year or so. Anything you can come up with. No detail too small. All right, beautiful?"

She said, "Sure Pat. Come by anytime. Don't bother to call. I'll be here."

We left unspoken any reference to the fact that we had just had sex, much less the question of whether it was to be a one-time event or the beginning of a genuine romance. I gave her a big hug and a kiss and said, "Don't you worry. Things are going to be fine. Patrick Brennan is on the case."

As I made my way down the long walkway to my car, I had to shake my head. I'd put on a happy face for Delilah, but the truth was that was only because I saw no point in letting on just how much trouble I figured she was in.

CHAPTER 12
MINGEE

Mingee came by my apartment for lunch the next day, Wednesday. She was happy to feed me all the information she had about how things were going with the sheriff and PA regarding the investigation, but she had no interest at this point in being seen with me in public by anyone remotely involved with law enforcement. Suddenly I was like Kryptonite to her.

"So Mingee," I said when she knocked on my door, "you remembered the way. Just like old times, huh?"

"Hah hah, you so funny, Patrick. Don't be getting ideas. It's not going to be like old times."

That was the problem with her. She could always read my mind.

"Okay, sorry. Bad joke. I do appreciate you coming by, really."

I grilled hamburgers for us out on my deck. I washed mine down with a Newcastle. She drank diet coke.

"So tell me. How goes the search for Francis Capella's killer?"

"Pretty much stuck in first gear at the moment. I mean, they like his wife for it. Actually they love her to death. Unfortunately they don't have enough evidence to ask for a search warrant for the residence, much less even dream about an indictment."

I said, "I'm convinced she didn't do it. You need to take a harder look at the housekeeper."

"Not me. I'm not assigned to the investigation."

"Well, you ought to be. Why don't you push for it?"

"No way I'm getting near it, Patrick. They know about our history, and your frequent visits to the Capella residence have not gone unnoticed. They're not morons. They can put two and two together. Your interest in the grieving widow has clearly gone beyond the professional."

I chose not to respond to her remark, and for a while we sat in silence.

Finally Mingee said, "Anyway, they've interviewed Lourdes. Her story checks with what Mrs. Capella told us. She was off the day Frank died. She has no conceivable motive. As far as they're concerned she's in the clear. As for your little girlfriend, they're working overtime to tie her to Brad Johnson. Until they can she can rest easy. She's safe for the time being."

"Well, that's great news, Mingee. Tell them they need to drag Lourdes back in, and push her harder. I'm convinced she knows more than she's letting on."

Mai said, "So tell me the truth, Patrick. You sleeping with this woman?"

I weighed my answer for a few minutes, but then thought what the hell, it's a free country, right?

"We've been intimate, yes. Don't know where it's going."

She said, "Be very careful with that, Patrick. You are playing with fire. You never did have good sense, but this one could burn you badly. Play it straight, I'm warning you. Obstruction of justice is not something a licensed PI wants on his resume."

I answered, "Yeah, I'm sure you're right. That would be almost as bad as a law enforcement officer tampering with evidence." I let that little gem hang in the air long enough to achieve its full effect.

"Touché." she said, "Nevertheless, I'll say it one last time. Be very careful."

For the moment we let the subject drop. We finished our lunch and enjoyed a very nice conversation about all the very nice peripheral things going on in our lives. I asked after her parents, who were doing fine. She told me about her recent trip to Europe, which apparently had been great fun. Next she was planning a visit to her homeland, and of course she was very excited about that. We didn't discuss her current boyfriend. We didn't discuss my personal life, since I'd really not had one since Mai and I parted ways, and so the conversation devolved into the usual inconsequential small talk. Mostly we didn't discuss Delilah; there was an unspoken agreement between us to let that slide.

As she was leaving, however, I felt a compulsion to revisit the subject. I said, "Look, Mingee, just so you know. I haven't gone all wobbly and sentimental with this Delilah. It's still the same cynical self-serving Patrick you knew and loved. She is, if I can exonerate her, going to be one very well off lady. And she is gorgeous. And she is very nice. And she is the best lover I've ever had, present company excluded, of course. And I have become fond of her, very fond. And I believe she is innocent. And I intend to prove it. So I'm going to play this one out, Orange County Sheriff and Orange County PA be damned."

Mai just sort of stared at me for the longest time, with a strange expression I found impossible to read. Jealousy? Disappointment? Disgust? I cannot say to this day. All I know is what she said as we parted. "Well, thank you very much for that information, Patrick. I believe I feel much better."

CHAPTER 13
DEL

Thursday morning I called Delilah at 8 o'clock. She'd said not to bother, but I wanted to get clarity on the subject most interesting to me at the moment: sex. I wanted to give her a graceful exit in case our first time was also going to be our last.

When she picked up I said, "Good morning, Del, how you doing this fair morn?"

"Good morning. Okay, I guess."

"So listen, Del. About the other day. I feel I owe you an apology. I feel like maybe I took advantage of you and the, you know, the situation. That was entirely out of bounds. I'm sorry."

"We'll talk about that when you get here, Patrick. Have you had breakfast?"

"No, I thought I'd grab a quick bite on the way over."

She said, "Don't. I'll make us something here."

I said, "Okay, great. Thanks. See you in a few minutes."

As I drove down PCH I puzzled over Del's response to my apology, which I'd found enigmatic. Apparently the status of our romance was too complicated to discuss over the phone. I decided to take that as a hopeful sign.

When she opened the door to greet me, she was dressed in a white terry robe, trimmed and monogrammed in gold braid. I figured she'd been out at the pool, sunbathing.

She led me into the kitchen, where she had a regular spread laid out on the island bar. Bagels, lox, cream cheese, eggs Florentine and a giant platter of fresh fruit. She made us each a cappuccino and we enjoyed a leisurely breakfast. The conversation was polite but consisted of stilted small talk, as if we were a couple on a first date. There was a sense in the air that we were dancing around a couple of very large issues, which of course we were.

46

When we were finished, Del took my hand and led me once again up the white marble staircase to the place I wanted most to revisit: the master suite.

She sat me down on the edge of the bed and began to sort of pace back and forth in front of me.

Finally she said, "The thing is, Patrick, I told you when we first met that I loved Frank and I did, but as you know he was not the best husband to me."

I said, "I believe everybody in Newport knew that, Del."

"Hah. Well, yes. It was not as bad as all that. He liked to cultivate a reputation with everyone. Everyone but me, of course. I'm afraid I wasn't completely candid with you that first day we talked. The fact is he was on occasion unfaithful, and his cheating was taking a toll on our own love life. He was a very persuasive man, Frank. As we used to say back home, he could charm the bacon off a bashful pig. Added to that was the fact that his clients were usually attractive women who were in a vulnerable state of mind. I'm afraid he found it difficult to resist taking advantage."

"Like I took advantage of you."

She smiled at this remark, and paused for a moment, as if to formulate just the right words. "That's exactly what we need to discuss. The fact is you did not take advantage of me. I'm a big girl and I can take responsibility for my own actions. The fact is you are a nice man, much nicer than he ever was, and you've been very kind to me. The fact is, Patrick, I've fallen for you. And I need you to understand that it's not just my present circumstances. What I feel for you is genuine."

I said, "Those are the most welcome words I've ever heard, Del. The God's honest truth is that I'm falling for you as well. Falling hard."

She said, "But here's the deal, Pat. I was raised as a proper Christian girl, and my years in this hedonistic little corner of the world haven't erased that training. I'm not a player. If we are to have, to have something, I need to know it's based on real feelings. Not just lust, and not for God's sake pity. I don't want a shining knight rescuing this damsel in distress. I want your help, of course. I need it, desperately. But more importantly I want your love."

"You have my word, Delilah."

"Thank you, Patrick. And you have me."

With that she shrugged off her robe. I was expecting to see her bathing suit, but instead she was dressed in lace bra and panties revealing enough to make a Brazilian beach girl blush. She wriggled out of them with a few seductive motions, and we made love for the second time.

It was even better than the first. I swear that at the moment of consummation I would gladly have given away all my earthly goods to charity in gratitude to the good and loving God who had blessed me with such a gift. It was astounding to me that an affair with this woman had blossomed so rapidly, seemingly out of nowhere. But I wasn't asking any questions at this point; I was ready to roll with it.

* * *

Back on the pool deck, freshly showered and dressed, we got down to business. We sat side by side on a stone bench in the garden behind the pool. Delilah had a small notebook in her hand.

"So, Del," I asked her, "tell me about your husband's recent clients."

"Okay," she answered, "In the last year and a half he had just three. All women, of course. All three the wives of very wealthy men, naturally. All long term marriages. Right in Frank's sweet spot."

"All right. So run them down for me."

"Sure. First, we have Macy Niyad, wife of Dr. Brian Niyad. You may have heard of him. He's a well-known plastic surgeon here in Newport."

"Not really."

"Well, there's no reason you would have, I guess. But in our social circle he's quite the celebrity. He's the best there is. UCLA Med School home grown hero. Half the women I know have his breasts. The standard joke is that maybe only God can make a tree, but when it comes to boobs Brian Niyad can go Him one better. Of course, he does it all. Face lifts, tummy tucks, fannies, you name it."

"I see. Okay. These going to be in chronological order, by the way?"

"Not really. I've arranged them more by how angry they appeared to be with my husband, based on our conversations, Frank and I, and how likely they are in my opinion to be capable of murder. Besides, the cases overlapped some."

"Okay. Good."

"Frank did really well for Macy. She got the house, all her personal possessions, of course, which included a ton of jewelry, and half a million in cash. Plus alimony. Plus half the practice."

I pushed a soft whistle through my lips. "Hmm. Nice."

"Yeah. Nice. She's set. But trust me, Brian is doing fine. He has plenty left over. His practice brings in boatloads. More than he can spend. He's also a very hot commodity on the market, if you know what I mean, now that he's single. I hear he's going through the ladies at a very healthy clip. I've never been a patient, but I've met him a couple of times. Very nice gentleman, soft spoken. I can't imagine he could be involved in harming anyone."

"Yeah, well you never know. I've been surprised before in my line of work. We'll see. I'll check him out. So who's next up on the hit parade?"

Del glances briefly at her notes.

"Next would be Erik Nordstrom, or rather Mrs. Erik Nordstrom. You know, the Metatronics guy."

I did know. Nordstrom's story is famous, a real geek rags-to-riches tale. He was an electronics whiz at Stanford in the early days of the computer revolution. He founded Metatronics out of the back of a Volkswagen microbus along with his wife, Sarah, and grew it into the biggest chip company this side of Silicon Valley. It specializes in DSP's, digital signal processors, the chips that run televisions, smart phones, GPS receivers and the like.

He is generally considered to be one of the richest men in the country. His company is headquartered in Irvine but owns fabrication plants around the world, including Mexico, Singapore and China.

Now we are talking real money. He has to be worth billions. My God, that must have been a nice payday for Frank.

I said, "Sure, I am familiar. That must have been one very sweet deal your husband got for the little lady. Not to mention himself."

Del reached up and swiped off her Maui Jims, looked me in the eyes and said, in a quiet and very serious tone, "He killed it, Pat. Absolutely killed it."

"I don't even want to know. And so how did Mr. Nordstrom take the news?"

"He was pissed off, I can tell you that for nothing. It wasn't the money. He's got more than enough of that, and Sarah had been with him from the beginning so it didn't seem he begrudged her a fair share. It was more the public disclosure of his personal finances and those of the company. Added to that he's apparently an over the top control freak and does not handle rejection well."

"I see. So it was his wife that wanted out?"

"Right."

At this point Del stood up and said, "I'm getting cold. Mind if we go inside?"

She was right. By now it was late March, and spring had officially begun, but it had rained the night before and the air was still unsettled. The wind off the ocean had grown steadily stronger with the day and it had become chilly as we talked.

Once inside we migrated back to the kitchen bar. She offered me a cappuccino but I was coffee'd out. She excused herself to return upstairs and brush her hair out. While she was gone I was thinking to myself that so far things didn't look promising. The two persons of interest she'd provided me didn't appear to be all that promising, at least for our purposes. But then, you never know.

When she returned I asked her, "So. Tell me about number three."

"Sure. That would be Angelina Aguilar. Her husband, Marcelo, owns Eagle Homebuilders."

"Okay. I've heard of that company."

"Yes, I'm sure you have. He's the biggest developer in Orange County. With Angelina it was a real Pygmalion story. He brought her up from a little godforsaken village in Mexico. She was less than half his age at the time. She was very beautiful, but pretty rough around the edges. He hired an English tutor to teach her to speak without an accent and teach her proper etiquette, bought her the best clothes, showered her with jewelry, the whole bit. It was a real fairy tale for a while, but eventually and predictably she became Americanized and as jaded and spoiled as the rest of us girls in Southern California."

I was too smart to bite on that. I said, "Hah. Very funny."

"Aren't I? So after time she became a little weary of living under Marcelo's thumb. From what Frank told me he kept her on a very short leash. She was like the proverbial bird in a gilded cage. Somewhere along the line a friend to whom she'd been complaining gave her my husband's name, and the rest is history."

I said, "Yeah, I can only imagine."

"Yes you can. My husband was only too happy to introduce the girl to the wonders of the California family law legal system, with its many splendid benefits for mistreated spouses like herself. Unfortunately, I'm fairly certain that he also introduced her to the wonderful world of love-making with Francis Capella, who by the way I can tell you was a really wonderful love maker. He denied it, but everyone was saying it was true and by this time I was tired of his denials."

"Ouch."

"Ouch doesn't begin to cover it, Pat. It was a real problem for me, obviously. It came very close to blowing up our marriage. But then the case was over, and she went back to Mexico with her pot of gold. Frank like literally got down on his knees and begged me to reconcile. He swore he would never be unfaithful again. We were working our way back to some sort of rebirth of our relationship. What really makes me sad, and I shouldn't even share this with you, but the fact is the night before Frank died when we made love it was the first time in months. I was hopeful we really were getting our marriage back on track."

I said, "Jeez, Del, I'm sorry. That's really very sad."

"Yes. But you know, the truth is I was kidding myself. I mean, I loved him, but he was like never going to change. I can't say where our relationship would ever have ended up."

I decided we had gone down this maudlin road about as far as was wise. I needed to refocus the discussion on the issue at hand.

I said, "So tell me your thoughts on this Marcelo character. Can you see him clipping Frank?"

"Oh, I don't know. If he ever found out that my husband slept with Angelina, Frank kept that information from me. If he did, that Latin *machismo* thing might have kicked in. I did hear a rumor that he publicly threatened to kill Frank, but I can't confirm that."

"Okay. Thanks. Looks like I have my work cut out for me."

As I left, I felt the usual sort of ambivalence that had plagued me from the beginning with this case. On the one hand, I had a short list of men who conceivably could have had Capella killed, and I was going to be doing my due diligence to run them down. On the other hand, I was dealing with three very rich men, all having much to live for, and none of whom I could imagine taking the extraordinary risk of committing or soliciting murder. I could see it would be very tough hanging a homicide charge on any of them.

CHAPTER 14
BRIAN NIYAD, M.D.

I decided to take them in the order that Del had given them to me, so first up was Brian Niyad. His office was in South Laguna, at the South Coast Medical Center. I called the next morning, and was able to set an appointment for that afternoon, after his morning surgeries.

I was greeted by his receptionist, a pretty twenty-something blonde number that looked as if she might have taken out part of her salary in trade. She'd left the top buttons of her blouse undone, in case anybody missed the point.

I couldn't help but wonder if, well, you know.

When she opened the door to the doctor's office he was standing behind his desk. He came around to shake my hand, and as she closed the door behind me I nodded my head in the young lady's direction.

"Very nice," I said, "Samples of your work?"

He just smiled.

He was dressed in jeans, a white knit shirt, a blue blazer and a pair of blue and yellow Nike running shoes. He was taller than I'd pictured, and thin almost to the point of gauntness. He appeared to be mid-forties to fifty years of age. He wore wire-rimmed eyeglasses that along with his prematurely gray hair made him look like an accountant.

What he did not look like, at the moment, was a plastic surgeon; nor did his office look like that of a physician. It was expensively and tastefully furnished in leather couch and armchair. Wool Berber carpet covered the floor. Original pieces of modern art hung on the walls. Bookcases completely covered one wall, and while the subject matter appeared eclectic, a casual glance revealed not a single medical text. There was none of that silly business with plastic models of body parts or garish anatomical charts. A single framed diploma issued by UCLA hung discreetly on the wall behind his chair, the only indication of his profession.

He slouched as we spoke, leaning against the front of his desk in an annoyingly regal posture of relaxation, arms folded against his chest. No surprise there, I guess. A doctor of his standing would be accustomed to being shown a great deal of deference.

"So," he said after I'd introduced myself and the appropriate pleasantries had been exchanged, "I'm curious. Why does a private investigator working for Cal Life want to talk to me?"

I said, "I'm looking into the death of Francis Capella. I believe you two were acquainted."

A pained expression flickered briefly across his face. "Acquainted is not the word I'd use, but yes, I knew the bastard. What are you looking into, exactly? It was an accident, right?"

I didn't want to mention the GHB thing, as it had yet to become public knowledge. I said, "Probably. We just want to be sure. There's a large sum of money involved."

"I see. Double indemnity."

"Right. You catch on quick. So we were just wondering, my friends and I at Cal Life. Any chance you might have had a hand in his death?"

He looked stunned for just a moment, but recovered quickly and laughed at my question. He said, "Jesus, Brennan, you don't beat around the bush, do you?"

Actually, most times I do beat around the bush, quite a bit, but something told me the direct approach was the way to go with him. I was curious to see if he could take a punch.

I said, "They don't pay me by the hour."

"You cannot be serious. How the hell could I make his Porsche fly off a cliff?"

"Good question. Honestly, I haven't a clue. We're just looking at motive right now, and we figure you have a pretty good one. He worked you over pretty well, I hear."

"You heard right. That he did. I guess there were times when I wouldn't have minded killing him. I know my own attorney would have been happy to. He pretty much got chewed up and spit out by the son-of-a-bitch. But despite it all you have to feel bad for the poor sod. I had a Porsche Turbo once myself. Around here they're a dime a dozen, of course. Thing was wicked fast, but it rode like a Conestoga wagon and was borderline dangerous. I drive an Aston Martin now. It's a really sweet ride. It's much more impressive to the ladies and you don't have to be a goddamn professional race car driver to keep it on the pavement."

I said, "Yeah, I hear that's a real nice automobile. Very classy. James Bond and all. Out of my price range, unfortunately."

He was by now sitting on the corner of his desk, one foot on the floor and one dangling in the air, arms splayed and hands palm down along the wooden edge. The subject matter of our conversation hadn't affected his composure in the slightest.

He slipped off the blazer and threw it onto the seat of his chair. I noticed that he had a tattoo, of all things, on the upper part of his left arm. It was nothing special, an anchor overlaid with a heart, the kind of thing you see on retired sailors all the time. A scroll with the name 'Suzy' ran below the whole bit.

I couldn't resist asking. I said, "That's a bit of a cultural disconnect, isn't it? You don't see many doctors with tattoos."

He laughed. "No, you're right. You don't. Fortunately for me, my professional reputation allows me to get away with a few eccentricities."

"How'd you come by it?"

"Very honestly, I can assure you. I did a tour in the Navy on the USS Independence, back in the day. Vietnam and all that. They put me through medical school, the Navy, and in return I gave them eight years of active duty."

I said, "I see."

He pointed to the tat with his right forefinger and said, "This is the result of a night of bar-hopping in Olongapo, lovely little vacation spot outside the U.S. Naval base at Subic Bay in the Philippines. Talk about your epic hangovers. I've thought about having it removed, but there's a certain sentimental attachment, I find. Those were good years, believe it or not."

I said, "Yeah, I've heard it was a real party. And this Suzy, she was the love of your life, was she?"

"Well, she was that night, apparently."

My turn to laugh. "I get the picture. But back to our friend Mr. Capella. He cost you a ton of dough. That's a pretty good motive for revenge."

"I suppose so, if you're the vengeful type. Actually, I'm not. I was angry at the time. The divorce was a mutual thing. Macy and I had pretty much run our course. It was going to be a nice, amiable little affair until that bastard got involved and got her all worked up. After that they went for my jugular, the two of them. But I'm over it. We were married a long time. She got more than I thought was fair, but the truth is I'm not exactly hurting. I have more left than I will ever spend, even if I shut down my practice today. And I'm not doing that. So no, Mr. Brennan, I did not arrange Francis Capella's death. But I freely admit I certainly did welcome it, although I do feel bad for his lovely young wife."

"I see. That's very sporting of you."

"Thanks. You know the old joke about why divorces cost so much, right?"

"Because they're worth it."

"Right. I really am enjoying my new found freedom. Macy and I were at the point where we were absolutely smothering each other. Since the whole mess has been over, I've rediscovered my *joie de vivre*. Now that I think of it, I should probably have sent Capella a thank you note."

"Well, too late for that I'm afraid, no postal deliveries to his present address, but I am very happy to hear that you're in a good place."

"I'll tell you another thing. Just between us girls. I haven't gotten this much tail since my days in the Philippines. You have any idea how easy it is to get laid by young and beautiful women here on the Orange Coast if you happen to be an unmarried and successful plastic surgeon?"

"It pains me to even contemplate that question, Doc, but I do thank you for your time and your candor."

As I was turning to leave he said to me, "Hey Brennan, you ever hear the one about the man who felt sick and made an appointment with his doctor? Doc runs some tests and has him come back in a week. When he does the doctor tells him he has good news and bad news. The man says, 'tell me the bad news first.' The doctor says, 'You have a terminal illness and will be dead in six months.' The man says, 'my God, please tell me the good news.' Doc says, 'You saw my gorgeous blonde receptionist, right? I'm screwing her!' Funny, huh?"

I shook my head, smiled and said "Very funny indeed. You should do standup."

As I opened the office door to leave I turned to his receptionist, gave her a big smile and nodded good-bye. I started to ask her how many times she'd heard that corny joke, but thought better of it.

It seemed to me that Del was right. He was a pretty regular guy and a pretty laid back kind of dude. Maybe a tad arrogant for my taste, but it was hard to imagine him harming anyone or anything. He was clearly more interested in chasing girls than seeking revenge. Strike one.

After I left his office it occurred to me, as it does from time to time. Mother was right. I should have gone to medical school.

CHAPTER 15

ERIK NORDSTROM

It took me almost a week to arrange an appointment with Mr. Nordstrom. In the meantime I continued my visits to Delilah, and we continued to make very satisfying love on an almost daily basis. It felt a little weird being in Capella's bed, not to mention being in his widow. Somehow I was able to deal with it. I never spent the night, however, as that seemed just a tad inappropriate.

We had the house to ourselves now that Frank's kids had sacked Lourdes.

I didn't hear any more from Mai. I figured she was aware of my activities, as law enforcement was surely keeping tabs on Del, and I figured she was none too happy about the situation. What the hell, she had her chance.

I was beginning to think the whole thing was going to blow over, the investigation I mean. They had the GHB, but without a way to connect it to Del it meant nothing. They were at a dead end. It even looked as if Cal Life was going to be on the hook for the whole bit, and I allowed myself thoughts of a more permanent relationship with my lover, her and her five million dollars.

I was determined to see my end of the investigation through to the end, though. As I told Del, it would still be great if I could remove the cloud of suspicion from over her head.

* * *

The world headquarters of the Metatronics Corporation occupy the top three floors of a luxe high rise office building in Newport Center. Nordstrom's secretary kept me cooling my heels for an hour and a half before ushering me into his presence.

His suite occupied the entire top level. Floor to ceiling glass windows gave him a 360 degree view from his desk of Balboa Island to the south, including his splendid dockside residence and 100 foot plus yacht, John Wayne Airport to the north, including his white and gold Gulfstream emblazoned with the Metatronics logo, and the Santa Ana mountains to the northeast. It was a very impressive setup.

His appearance was well-matched to his surname. He was of medium height, and athletically built. He had high cheekbones, blue eyes and buzz cut blonde hair. He was dressed in a very expensive looking suit, I'm guessing bespoke Savile Row. Underneath he was sporting an Egyptian cotton custom-tailored shirt, open at the collar. The office was cold, and I could hear the A/C working hard in the background. There was a gray haze of cigarette smoke, and I noticed a pack of Marlboro Reds lying on the corner of his desk.

His face wore a perpetual salesman's smile. He extended a hand and shaking it was like reaching into a frozen vise.

He said to me as I flexed my fingers, trying to reestablish blood flow, "Sorry to keep you waiting. Been on an international conference call, kicking some serious ass. I'm having a hell of a time with our fab in China. The indigenous out there could not organize a pissing contest in a beer factory, I swear. You hear a lot about how they're coming on strong over there, but I'm here to tell you they have a long way to go.

"But I digress. What is it I can do for you, exactly, Mr. Brennan? They tell me you're with an insurance company?"

"Sort of. I'm a private investigator, actually. I'm looking into the death of Francis Capella, Mr. Nordstrom."

"Call me Erik. Everybody does."

"Okay. I'm looking into the death of Francis Capella, Erik."

"What does that have to do with me? He died in an automobile accident, right?"

"Well, or so it seems. An automobile crash, certainly. The insurance company I represent wants to assure itself that it *was* an accident. The man had a lot of enemies."

"No shit."

"Right. No shit," I laughed. "Just routine of course. Nobody really believes the accident was any more than just that. I'm checking off boxes, is all. Pro forma sort of thing. They're looking at cutting a very large check, my clients. They always find that painful and repugnant."

"I see. Of course."

"And so we're just interviewing some of the people who might have liked to see him dead. At least those with a recent cause to wish him dead, to be exact. That would include people like his wife, for example, and, well, you."

It was his turn to laugh. "Hah. You have me there. It certainly would include me. I was overjoyed at the news. Absolutely made my day. As Mark Twain once said of a dead enemy, 'I did not attend his funeral but I certainly approved of it.'"

"I thought that may be the case. That Twain was a real card, by the way. He beat you up pretty badly, I hear. Capella, I mean. Mrs. Nordstrom, the ex-Mrs. Nordstrom, got a boatload I'm told."

"Whoever told you that knew whereof they spoke. That's not the part that pisses me off, though. Sarah was with me from the very beginning, the early days back at Stanford. She stuck with me through some hard times. She deserved every penny. Trust me, she earned it. I'm not an easy man."

I said, "Judging by your reputation, you speak euphemistically."

"You don't get to be a billionaire by being a nice guy, Brennan."

"Yeah, that's what my mother told me. I guess that's why I'm not. A billionaire, I mean. Call me Pat, then."

"Okay, Pat, I will do that."

"So what is it that does piss you off, Erik?"

"It was the way the greasy little bastard dragged my personal finances and Metatronic's into the proceedings and thus into the public domain. In business, my friend, information is like gold. Doubly so in the chip business, where the competition is especially nasty. I had the best lawyers money could buy but the underhanded little prick got around them. Spilled a lot of proprietary information into the press. That hurt."

"Yeah, I can see that it would. Say, uh, I hope you don't mind my asking. He had a reputation for seducing his clients."

"No worries. Sarah has too much class and too much intelligence to have fallen for his line of guinea bullshit. Berkeley gal. Very sharp."

"Good. That's a relief, then, at least."

"You're a funny guy, Pat."

"I try. It's a depressing line of work, investigation."

"I can imagine. Anyway, speaking of work, I have some of my own

I need to get back to. Any more questions?"

"Just one, I suppose. You didn't happen to have had a hand in arranging that accident, then, did you, Erik?"

He pursed his lips as if thinking exactly how to answer, and then resumed the wide smile.

He said, "Pat, I graduated Valedictorian from the most prestigious prep school in the great state of California, at age fifteen. Got a perfect score, 1600, on the SATs. I was accepted into Stanford University at age sixteen, from which I graduated with degrees in physics and electrical engineering in three years. At age twenty, I was doing leading edge research into quantum phenomena in solid state materials. I founded this company at twenty three and by thirty was a billionaire, with too many patents and awards to count. I mention all this not to brag, but simply to make the point that I am not a stupid man."

"I never doubted your intelligence, Erik."

"Good. And since it would be a very stupid thing to do for a man in my position, with what I have to lose, to commit murder for the purpose of achieving a very pointless and futile revenge, I can assure you I had nothing to do with it. I'm a businessman, Pat, not a gangster."

"A very ruthless businessman, to be fair."

"Comes with the territory, my friend. I crush my competitors with pricing, efficiency and superior technology. Much more effective, not to mention satisfying, than violence."

"You have a point, Erik," I said by way of making my exit. "Thanks for your time."

"No problem."

As I made my way through his outer office, I nodded farewell to his secretary and sighed to myself. Strike two.

CHAPTER 16

CLUB NEON

I was left with my last person of interest, and really the only one who in my judgment held any promise as a potential murderer. Marcelo Aguilar, that would be. I was still trying to set a meet with him when Mai finally got in touch with me again. Her call came early and woke me.

I grabbed my phone off the nightstand, saw it was she calling, and said, "Good morning. I thought I might never hear from you again."

I said it with a smile in my voice, but there was none in hers. She sounded as solemn as an undertaker. "Patrick, we need to talk."

"Sure, darlin', what's your pleasure?"

I was expecting her to suggest the Au Lac, or maybe one of the Vietnamese coffee shops she liked to frequent. So it came as a shock when she said, "Downtown, Pat. Why don't you come on up to headquarters. Come to my office."

Jesus, I thought. She'd spent the last couple of weeks trying to put as much distance between us as possible, and suddenly she wants to see me in her office? This was not going to be a social visit. This was business. This was serious. I jumped out of bed, had a quick breakfast and a shower, and headed up to Santa Ana.

* * *

When I arrived at Mai's office, which is actually a cubicle in a large glass-partitioned room of cubicles, I noticed two unsettling things. First, she was dressed in uniform, her service Glock .40 strapped to her waist. Second, she was not alone. A gentlemen with whom I was not familiar, also in uniform, was seated to her side. Neither of them rose to greet me; neither of them was smiling.

She said, "Patrick, thanks for coming. Meet my colleague, Lieutenant Doherty."

I nodded and said, "Howdy."

He nodded in return, and then turned and nodded to Mai. She said to me, "We'll be wanting to do this in one of our interrogation rooms, if you don't mind. This is going to be on the record."

"Sure, Officer Nguyen, whatever you like."

They led me down the hallway, around a corner or two, and into a section of the floor lined with numbered doors, each with small rectangular windows near the top of wire-reinforced and frosted glass. They chose room five, a very nice little cubby with lovely institutional mint green walls and classically simple gray metal table and chairs. The obligatory panel of one-way glass occupied one of the end walls. A video camera was mounted conspicuously above it. A tape recorder sat on the tabletop.

They took seats on one side, and gestured for me to take a load off on the other.

I said, "Gee, I feel like I'm on the ID Channel."

Doherty said the only thing he was to utter during the entire course of the interview, "If I was you, Brennan, I'd put a lid on the wisecracks. We're not in the mood."

I said, "So what's this all about, Mingee? What's up?"

She said, "What's up, Patrick, is that we have tentatively established a link between your little friend Delilah and Brad Johnson. I take it I don't need to elaborate on the ramifications thereof."

"What sort of link?"

"Ever since we identified the GHB we've had officers reviewing surveillance video from every bar, nightclub and restaurant in Newport, on the off chance we might find some tape starring Brad Johnson and your girlfriend. It was a long shot, and a really massive undertaking. But damned if we didn't hit pay dirt a couple of days ago. We have the two of them together at Club Neon, on Lido, two months before Capella died."

I had heard of the Neon, though I had never been. It wasn't my style, but it was very popular among the clubbers in Newport. A great place to get hooked up with girls and/or drugs was the word. Just the sort of place you would expect to find Longboard, of course, but I found it hard to feature Delilah there.

Mingee said, "But now to the reason you are here, Patrick."

63

Her hand hovered over the tape machine at this point. She punched a button and it began to spin.

She continued, "I can tell you that Tanaka is very close to a decision to indict Mrs. Capella for the premeditated murder of her husband. A grand jury has been impaneled and the case is being prepared. In view of your, uh, intimate friendship with this woman, I have a question for you, and I want you to consider very carefully before answering. I also have a caution for you, before you do. If the PA gets the slightest whiff that you are in any way concealing information you may have as a result of your relationship, of an inculpatory nature, he will not hesitate to bring you along for the ride, on charges of obstruction of justice at a minimum and possibly accessory after the fact. That said, I want to ask you, Patrick, on the record: Do you have anything you'd like to tell us?"

My head was spinning at this point, as I tried to digest this new information and assess its impact. There were so many angles to look at. Life had been seeming so simple.

I finally answered her, "As God is my witness I still believe that Delilah is innocent. I swear I have no information that inclines me to think otherwise. You are right, of course, that I know her, that I know her well. I'm convinced she is not capable of murder, and especially not the murder of her husband. As to the GHB, I admit I have no good explanation. Likewise her contact with Brad Johnson, if in fact that is proven. Obviously I will be asking Del why she would be seeing this character. I assume that you would not have told me about the tape you have if you didn't want her to know."

Mai said, "That's true. Go ahead and ask her. We will certainly be doing likewise in short order."

With that the interview was over and I was unceremoniously escorted from the building. I had some serious thinking to do. I needed more than ever to speak with Aguilar. But first things first.

CHAPTER 17

DELILAH

Delilah is naked. She lies supine beneath me. I kneel astride her. Her belly glistens with perspiration into which I lazily trace patterns with my fingers. Her eyes are closed, her breathing shallow. We have just finished making love.

I have not yet spoken of my conversation earlier in the day with Mai, for two reasons. Principally and most importantly is the fact that such a conversation almost certainly would have spoiled the sex. But I also am interested in whether Del will admit voluntarily to having met with Brad.

I lowered my head near her ear and whispered, "And so, Delilah, is there anything, anything at all you would like to tell me?"

She gave me an expression as if to indicate she was completely nonplussed by my question, but not before I caught a flicker of guilt cross her face.

She said, "What do you mean, Pat?"

"Oh, I don't know, sweetie. I've just been wondering if you maybe are not being completely, uh, forthcoming with me. I'm asking myself if you're holding out on me?"

"About what, Pat? What can you possibly be getting at?"

"I don't know. Let's say for example about Brad Johnson. About you not having any recent contact with him. That's still your story, correct?"

The color drained instantly from her face and she rolled over from beneath me onto her stomach, her head turned away from me, the side of her face flat against the mattress, her eyes closed.

I slapped her hard across her bottom. "Goddamn it, Del, you promised to be completely honest with me. That's the only way I can help, and trust me, you need help. They had me up to Santa Ana yesterday, to tell me they have video of you and Brad at the Neon. That changes everything,

Del. Here I was thinking you were probably clear, and instead I get completely blindsided by this happy news. I really had no good way to react. I felt like a complete fool."

"Sorry."

"It looks to me like you can expect to be arrested within the next couple of days."

She has nothing further to say. She simply lies under me sobbing. Without thinking about it, I find myself massaging the hand mark I've left on her bum.

"So, now, Del, you want to tell me about the meeting with Longboard? What was that all about? Scoring a little GHB, were you then? Or was it just a social visit? Catching up with an old friend, that sort of thing?"

She finally said, in a small pitiful little voice, "I knew that was what you'd think. I knew no one would believe me. That's why I couldn't bring myself to tell you. That club is complete chaos. It's like a sea of bodies in there and very dimly lit. I was sure we would never be noticed."

"You were right, you weren't. Sheriff's people went through all the video tape of all the clubs in Newport on the off chance. You got unlucky. Very unlucky. So tell me your story, girl. It had better be a good one."

"After the first girl filed a complaint against Brad, her story gave the police cause for a search warrant, with which they'd caught him completely unawares. And subsequently, of course, they discovered his tapes. It was not a pretty picture. He knew he was in real trouble and was expecting to be arrested at any time. I was the first person he called. He had no money, and he knew he needed a lawyer. He was hoping that I could maybe persuade Frank to represent him pro bono, you know, for old times' sake. Criminal law was way outside the area of my husband's practice of course, and anyway there was no way Frank would ever want his name associated with a child rapist. But I felt like I owed it to Brad to give him the bad news in person."

"For old times' sake?"

"I don't need sarcasm right now, Patrick. I know it was stupid."

"Stupid doesn't begin to describe it, sweetheart."

"I know. But at this point Frank was very much alive and I had never even heard of GHB."

"Okay, okay. Jesus, what a mess."

I rolled off Delilah and off the bed and began to get dressed. She did the same. Eventually we ended up back in the kitchen, sitting on stools at the bar. The mood was glum. There was no conversation between us for probably twenty minutes, as we each sat alone with our thoughts. The situation for Delilah was dire, of course, but also pretty much black and white. My situation was a little more complicated.

I began to work through in my mind the ramifications and possibilities attached to the present circumstances, with regards to my own personal position. There was no question that finding that coffee mug and turning it over to Mingee may turn out to have been the biggest blunder of my young life. Had I not done so Capella's death would have been written off as an accident, fortunate or unfortunate depending on your point of view, and Del would be in the clear and on the receiving end of a five million dollar check, set for life. I wouldn't have minded going for a ride on that train.

Of course, I had no way of knowing we'd be falling in love, and as a matter of fact we probably would not have except for the circumstances of the sheriff's investigation and the effect it had on her.

At any rate, that was all water under the bridge. The question for me now was what would happen going forward. There was the hope and very real possibility that if Delilah ended up going to trial she'd be acquitted. In that event she could still collect at least two and a half million. Would she still love me? Probably. Neither she nor anyone else outside Mai's department knew about my role in providing the evidence that compelled the coroner to rule Capella's death a homicide.

They had motive, opportunity, a body and a murder weapon, but it was still a largely circumstantial case. She would no doubt make a very sympathetic defendant. Still, I could not be optimistic. The Club Neon video was really a killer. My best bet was to find whoever could conceivably have killed Frank, if indeed such a person existed. That would open up a whole new world of possibilities for me.

Finally, I broke the ice. I said, "Del, I need a drink, a big one. I suggest you join me."

She said, "Patrick, its three o'clock in the afternoon. And you know I don't drink."

"It's five o'clock in Dallas, and I believe this is an excellent time for you to start. As for me, I'll take a double Johnny Black, please. On the rocks. Pour yourself a glass of wine."

Del was like a whipped puppy at this point. Her shoulders sagged, her head hung and her overall body language suggested weakness, tiredness and defeat. I felt really bad for her. These past weeks had taken a bigger toll on her than I'd imagined.

"Okay," she said, in a low whisper.

"Good girl. Trust me, a little alcohol will make us both feel better."

As she prepared our drinks she said over her shoulder, "So what do we do now, Pat?"

"Good question. As for you, like I said before you need to lawyer up and lawyer up fast. And when they question you, say nothing. Absolutely nothing. I'm encouraged by the fact Tanaka has impaneled a grand jury. That tells me he's unsure of the strength of his case against you and wants cover in case it goes south on him. It's all circumstantial, after all. And unless they have video showing Brad actually handing you GHB, the fact that you happened to be in a club at the same time means nothing. You have a valid explanation for that. And I'm pretty sure Mai would have told me if such tape existed. Tanaka's famous for being very cautious about protecting his win streak. He may be waiting for more evidence to turn up."

"I don't have much money left for an attorney."

"Yeah, I've thought about that. I've got some savings, but nothing like you're going to need. We have to get you some top flight talent. Here's the way I figure it. If you go to trial, or I guess *when* you go to trial, this is going to be a major story. It has all the elements the media love. A wealthy but highly unpopular, unfaithful and some would say unscrupulous husband, a young beautiful widow, a spectacular and mysterious death. Sex, lies and videotape. You are going to be a star, whether you like it or not. I'm pretty certain any number of top defense attorneys from around the country will be queuing up to represent you free of charge, just for the publicity."

"I hope you're right, Pat, but God I hate this. I'm a very private person."

"I know, sweetie, I know. Anyway, for me the priority is to find out who actually drugged your husband. I know you're innocent, so there has to be someone out there who isn't. I can't say I like Niyad or Nordstrom for it, so that leaves me Aguilar."

I decided to spend the night with Delilah. I could see that she was fragile and in need of moral support. As it turned out, I was wrong about our friend Mr. Tanaka. That afternoon was the last time ever that we made love. They came for her early the next morning.

CHAPTER 18
DIGITALE MOTRONIK ELECTRONIK

I was having trouble setting a meeting with Marcelo Aguilar for the time being. Delilah was still being processed in the Sheriff's intake facility and was unavailable. So I decided to pay a visit to the dealer that sold Frank his Porsche. I was still chewing on what Archie Fenner had said, about the engine on his car cutting out.

They tell me that one out of every ten Porsches produced is sold in Southern California. Makes sense, I guess, what with the freeways, the weather and the money, not to mention the crazy-for-cars culture. Certainly not the least of the many beneficiaries of this splendid business is the Newport Auto Center, seller of fine motor cars including Audi, Bentley and Porsche, dealer of multiple Porsche Carreras to the late great Francis Capella.

N.A.C. is located on the prosperous strip of PCH that passes through the Newport Harbor area, just to the south of Fashion Island and Newport Center, a short drive down the highway from Costa Mesa.

The service manager turned out to be a guy named Wolfgang Reichert, a tall tanned gentleman with long coiffed blonde hair, dressed in an expensive-looking suit and tie, the latter embroidered with a dozen or so of the miniature heraldic badges that represent Porsche's logo. He spoke with a very slight German accent, just enough to let you know he's the real deal straight from Stuttgart, even if a couple decades removed, someone a Porsche fanatic can be comfortable putting his or her trust in. Right out of central casting, in other words.

He had an annoying habit of wearing designer sunglasses indoors, sweeping them off occasionally as he spoke so that you could see the sincerity in his eyes.

After the pleasantries were concluded I said, "I appreciate your time, Mr. Reichert. The reason I asked to see you is I'm investigating the death of Francis Capella. I believe he was a client of yours?"

DIGITALE MOTRONIK ELECTRONIK

"Everyone calls me Wolf. Yes, one of our best. Bought a new 911 every year, just like clockwork. Always the top models, with every trim and package available. He will be missed."

"Yeah, well, my sincere condolences for your loss."

He nodded and smiled in a way that told me he completely missed the sarcasm. I said, "The thing is, Wolf, I have a witness that swears the engine of Capella's car died for a few seconds immediately preceding his loss of control. If that happened, you know, out of the blue, I can see where such a thing could catch a driver off guard and cause an oversteer loss of control. So I'm wondering. What are the odds?"

"Zero, close enough. Absolutely unheard of, unless he ran out of gas."

"No, that didn't happen. The car was full, unfortunately. It had just been topped off. Obviously not helpful when it crashed."

"No, it wouldn't have been."

"So how about mechanical failure?"

"Out of the question. The Carrera's engine functions are controlled by a very sophisticated electronic module."

"Yeah? Tell me about that."

"All right. We call it DME, digital motor electronics. Not so much different than most cars built these days, except we feel ours is a bit more advanced. It uses multiple microprocessors that perform millions of calculations per second. Sensors feed them information on ambient air temperature and pressure, fuel flow, throttle position, engine RPM and about half a dozen other less obvious parameters that don't come to mind at the moment. The processors then use an internally programmed map to calculate very precise values for the optimum fuel and air flow, and also the proper spark timing. These modules are extremely reliable. They automatically reconfigure themselves in the event of any failures of data input, and default to a safe mode to keep the engine running under all conceivable circumstances.

"The only problem we've ever heard of is damage from an electrical surge caused by jump starting the vehicle with cheap cables, and that's maybe a handful of cases in the whole US in the last ten years. Mr. Capella's Porsche was only a few weeks old. The battery was brand new, and I can't imagine him buying anything cheap for his car. If he even owned jumper cables he would have bought them from our parts department."

I said, "In which case they sure as hell would not have been cheap."

Once again the humor was lost on him. "Right. And even if he did manage to drain his battery and then damage the electronics, there would have been a check engine light, which I very much doubt he would have ignored."

"I'll be damned. So where's this modern day wonder located?"

"In this case, it's under the driver's seat. Actually, we have a vehicle in for service at the moment that's very similar to Mr. Capella's. I believe you'll actually be able to see the unit on this one. Would you care for a look?"

"I would indeed."

The service area has perhaps fifteen bays on each side of a long central, brightly illuminated aisle. Besides the standard Snap-On roll cabinets, each bay is furnished with a complex array of electronic machinery that reminded me of a medical ICU. I could actually see my face reflected in the floor of white epoxy. It's as clean as a hospital ward and quiet as a cathedral, save for the occasional brief whisper of an air-driven torque wrench or a couple of engines ticking over in idle.

All but a few of the bays were occupied by a variety of Porsche models, some raised on lifts, some in varying degrees of disassembly. It was a model of Teutonic order. Technicians in white smocks labored over them in a well-rehearsed but unhurried pace. The whole ballet was televised via closed circuit to the customer waiting room.

Reichert guided me to a beautiful shiny black-on-black Carrera Turbo. Its sleek surfaces positively glowed under the strong fluorescent lighting.

"Christ," I said, as much to myself as anyone else, "What a sweet ride. I'm betting you strap this baby on you best have your ears laid back."

"It's a very high performance piece of machinery."

"Right. Like I said."

The driver's door was ajar, and the interior had been partially gutted. The driver's seat had been removed and stored on a platform against the wall, draped in plastic.

Reichert pointed to a metal box mounted on the floor, directly under the missing seat. It was about the size of a cigar box, the color of dull, unpolished steel and had a fat bundle of wrapped cables running from a cannon connector at the rear, through the floorboard and toward the business end of the vehicle.

He said, "There you have it, Mr. Brennan. The brains of the automobile, if you will. The technician is preparing to remove it. It's being sent out to an aftermarket third party facility to be flashed."

I asked, "What's that mean?"

"It means the map is being reprogrammed to give the car more performance. The factory is actually a bit conservative with their settings. There's always a margin for a more aggressive setup."

"Hmm. Yeah, I can see where a stock Turbo might not be fast enough for some."

This time he didn't miss it. "You didn't hear it from me, but off the record some of our customers have more money than sense."

"Hah. Right. And so, Capella's car, was it ever in for service from the time he bought it, Wolf?"

"I'm certain it wasn't. As I mentioned he had owned it for only a short time."

That wasn't the answer I was looking for, unfortunately, but there it was. I thanked him and walked out, got in my car and headed up the coast to Costa Mesa. It looked like I needed a new theory.

But when I got home my answering machine was blinking. It was Reichert asking me to give him a call.

"What's up, Wolf?" I asked when he picked up.

"I don't know if it's important, but you asked about the Capella vehicle being in for service. After you left I remembered that we had put it on the rack for a day prior to delivery to give it a thorough once over and make absolutely sure it was perfect. Mr. Capella was a very finicky man and our best customer. We did everything we could to make sure he never had any issues."

"Okay, thanks. Do you know which mechanic did the check? You have a name?"

"I do. John Zabriskie. Johnny Z, we called him. Great kid, real sharp tech. We sent him to Germany for factory training."

"Thanks. I'd love to have a word with him, if you don't mind."

"I wouldn't mind, but I'm afraid he no longer works here. He gave notice a few weeks back. We hated to lose him. His mother won a bunch of money in the lottery. He went crazy with the spending when he heard the news. Bought himself a motorcycle, a bunch of clothes and a big screen television. But then he moved back to help Mom manage the new nest egg. Somewhere in the Midwest. Illinois, I think it was."

"No kidding. Thanks."

CHAPTER 19
THE SANTA ANA WOMEN'S DETENTION FACILITY

Delilah's face is framed by a thick acrylic window. It's a surreal experience, seeing her this way, something I could never in a million years have imagined. She's a mess, a complete emotional wreck. Her face is pale but her cheeks are red from crying. The terror in her eyes is palpable. She looks like she hasn't slept in two days, which may very well be the case.

It was two days after they arrested her, the earliest she was allowed visitation. I was in Santa Ana again, except that this time it's the women's jail, which is clustered in the Civic Center.

Del is dressed in a standard issue jumpsuit. Orange is definitely not her color. I spoke to her by telephone.

She said, "My God Patrick, what's going to happen to me?"

"Dark days for sure, Del, but keep your chin up. I'm not a lawyer, obviously, but it looks to me like they've jumped the gun on this one. It's a political football, a ton of public interest, and I think they're feeling a lot of pressure to act. Tanaka, the DA, is one very ambitious, very devious son-of-a-bitch, believe me.

"But look, this is strictly a circumstantial case, and a weak one at that. They have motive and opportunity but they have no evidence to speak of. No direct evidence. I mean, you tried to help an old acquaintance. Piss-poor judgement, you would have to say, but not a crime. I can think of any number of ways GBH could have ended up in Capella's coffee, starting with Lourdes. Who, by the way has totally gotten a pass on this. As I see it they have way overreached.

"Speaking of lawyers, you need one. If this ever goes to trial the publicity is going to attract a bunch I'm pretty sure, but for now get yourself a public defender. And again, Delilah, I cannot emphasize this enough. *Say nothing*. Not a fucking thing, excuse the French."

"Okay, Patrick, thanks. I don't know what I'd do without you."

"You won't be needing to find out, I promise. Meantime, sit tight and let's see where this goes. I'll be visiting as often as I can, but right now my priority is Aguilar. He's our best last hope. If the bastard had a hand in this I'll nail him. I guarantee it."

* * *

No visit to downtown Santa Ana would be complete without a visit to Mai's office, and when I left Del I made the short walk to her office.

She was in a feisty mood. "Look who's come to visit. Patrick Brennan, of all people. How you doing, Pat? I'm really truly sorry we had to break up your party. Looks like you're going to have to find yourself a new playmate."

"Aw, don't go getting all sentimental on me now, Mingee. It doesn't become you. If I didn't absolutely know better I'd be thinking there was a bit of jealousy rearing its ugly head."

"Hah, you wish, sugar. The only ugly head around here is perched on your shoulders. I'm just happy you're no longer consorting with a murderer. That doesn't become you."

"Well see, that's where you are tragically mistaken, sweetie. Delilah is no murderer, and I intend to prove it. Tanaka doesn't have near enough evidence to indict her, much less convict her, and you know that as well as I. This is all just theater. This is going to blow up in his face. Maybe both of them."

"She's going to be arraigned shortly, Pat. He's just working through the paperwork. After that, assuming the judge agrees to bind her over, we'll see who is right."

"You know what blows my mind, Mai? There were two people who had an obvious ability to put GHB in Capella's thermos. Two. And yet you have completely discarded one of them as a possibility. You talk about a rush to judgement."

"Not true. We *are* looking to run Lourdes through the wringer, trust me. We just can't find her."

"You're kidding. She's disappeared?"

"Yep. In a puff of smoke. She was here on a green card. We're guessing she went back to Mexico."

"And that doesn't demonstrate consciousness of guilt to you?"

"Wouldn't go that far. She's been left out of work. She has no family here. It doesn't seem that unreasonable that she might pack it in. Besides, there's no indication she had any motive at all to harm Capella. He was her paycheck."

"For Christ's sake, Mai. Come on."

"Okay, okay. If I'm being honest, yes, it's a hole. It's giving Tanaka pause. We're looking hard, and talking to our Mexican counterparts. They are not famous for their enthusiasm, though, when it comes to helping with this sort of thing."

CHAPTER 20

MANNY

Manny rolled out from behind the counter the minute I walked in, a big grin on his face. "Hey Manny," I said, "you still hiding out from ICE?"

"You betcha, bro. How about you? You still cruising the high schools for dates?"

"Nah. Judge issued a restraining order…said one more time and I'm going away for good."

We both laughed. It felt like old times to be breaking each other's balls, and Manny wheeled his chair up to my side so I could reach down and give him a hug.

I said, "So how you doing, man? How's Olivia? How's Edward?"

"Both are fantastic. Olivia's fat and sassy as ever. Edward's a junior now, getting' straight A's. He's looking to go to grad school."

"Splendid."

"And so what you got in the briefcase, Pat? You bring old Manny some cash?"

"I wish. Just some tools of the trade. Cameras, recorders, the usual crap. I'm working the Capella case. Thought I'd get some pics of the car, if you don't mind."

"Not in the slightest. State boys are done with it."

It had been, what, five years now since Manny Bautista lost the use of his legs in an off-duty auto accident. He was a great cop. We played in a softball league together before that, cops, a few prosecuting attorneys and a PI here and there…all people from what you might call the extended law enforcement community.

Afterward, they gave him this job at the impound facility, which I always thought would creep me out under the circumstances, being around a bunch of wrecked cars. Didn't seem to bother Manny, though, except that the job offered little opportunity for advancement in rank, or over-time pay, and therefore he and Maria struggled somewhat to maintain their lifestyle.

His son, Edward, turned out to be a very gifted student, and when he was accepted to Princeton it was not looking too feasible for him to accept, despite a generous scholarship offer. So some of us guys on the team put together a fundraiser to put the kid over the top, one of the few decent things I've done in my life, and consequently Manny loves us like brothers.

It had been a while, and it was obvious that years in a wheelchair had taken their toll. Manny was balding, his face was doughy, and he was carrying maybe ten or fifteen extra kilos around the midsection. The lost hair was replaced by a scraggly beard, which was rapidly going grey. But the light still shined brightly in his eyes and that infectious laugh of his was alive and well. I had to wonder if I could deal with his situation half as well as he was.

"So Manny, did Mai mention I may be coming by?"

He shot me a wink and said, "Detective Nguyen, you mean? Yeah, she did warn me you might want to check out the Porsche that big time at-torney wasted himself in. Told me to watch you close and make sure you don't steal any of the furniture."

"Beautiful."

"Stopped by personally, as a matter of fact, and ain't she still a sweet little piece of ass? I can't believe you're not still with her."

"Respect, bro. Respect. But I do know what you mean. Sometimes I can't believe it myself."

"Yeah well, you always were a dumbass."

"Okay, funny man. Mind if I just take a look at the car?"

Manny tossed me a ring of keys and said, "Be my guest. The big one unlocks the main door to the warehouse. The small ones are numbered to match the storage pens."

"Thanks. Care to join me?"

"Gonna pass, bro."

I breathed a small sigh of relief. I had to ask for appearances' sake, but I really needed to be alone with Capella's vehicle.

I walked from Manny's office into the hallway leading to the storage area, a long straight featureless affair painted a depressing shade of gray. There are a couple of unmarked doors, a ladies' and men's and a half-open janitor's closet. At the end is a heavy metal door with a sign that reads: "Authorized Personnel Only. OC Sheriff."

The space on the other side is remarkably similar in size and layout to the service area at N.A.C., the main differences being that the vehicles residing here are in considerably poorer shape, and the bays they occupy are pens enclosed by chain link partitions and padlocked chain link doors. The lighting is dim, which makes the scene that much creepier.

Walking the center aisle between pens is a sad and grisly journey. They don't bring the fender benders here; this is a graveyard for fatal accident cases. Every mangled vehicle in the gallery has a horror story to tell, a tale of ineffable pain and the tragedy of lost lives. Most are liberally splashed with human blood. It's a gruesome picture.

Halfway down I spotted what I assumed must be Frank's Porsche, although it was tough to be sure. It was worse than I feared. It looked at first glance as if it had already been through a crusher. The pen was number thirteen, Frank's unlucky number.

I fumbled through the ring of keys to find the one that matched and unlocked the padlock. A standard issue 911 comes out of the factory at 177.1 inches, or just under fifteen feet. The pile of twisted metal I was looking at had been reduced to about eight. It clearly impacted tail first, just as Archie described. The engine assembly had been pushed forward, collapsing the passenger compartment to the point that the seats were crammed against the dashboard. The seats themselves were just skeletal metal and wire frames. Remnants of air bag material lay draped across them, badly scorched and melted into the springs. The leather upholstery had been completely consumed by fire. The front compartment lid had been blown open and forward, apparently by the exploding gas tank. There were just a few fragments of glass clinging to the window frames. The rear wheels must have come off in the impact; they were stacked in the corner, and the rear end was on blocks. Both doors had also been removed and lay in a pile in another corner. Reichert told me the car was silver, but you couldn't tell it by me; every surface I could see was black.

I saw that getting to the part I needed was going to be a challenge. The floorboard was folded into an A shape by the collision and the driver's seat remained firmly attached to it as it moved forward. I unlatched my briefcase and spread it open on the floor. My tool kit was wrapped in a towel. It consisted of a pair of channel lock pliers, a twelve inch pry bar, a pair of heavy-duty wire cutters and a crescent wrench. That last item was probably not going to do me much good; the bolts had probably all been fused to the frame by the heat of the explosion.

Using the pliers and wire cutters I was able to remove the springs and melted airbag material from the driver's seat bottom, exposing the box that housed the DME. It was scorched and covered with soot, but otherwise looked to be in surprisingly good shape. As I expected the four bolts used to secure it to the floorboard wouldn't budge, but eventually by using the pry bar and pliers I was able to twist the box off. I wrapped it in the towel and threw everything back into the briefcase. I wasn't sure what good it was going to do me or how it would help my investigation, but at least I had a souvenir to take home.

My hands were a sooty mess by now, so before leaving I stopped into the men's room to clean up, then wet a few paper towels to clean off the lock and keys, and the handle of the main door.

I left everything in storage pen thirteen pretty much as I'd found it.

I ducked back into Manny's office on the way out to say good-bye.

Manny asked, "So did you get some good pics, Pat?"

"Yeah, sure did. A bunch of them. You want a set?"

"Gonna pass yet again, bro." He tapped the side of his head. "Got a full set up here."

"I hear you. Take care. Love to Olivia."

"You bet."

CHAPTER 21
MARCELO AGUILAR

I had come to realize that the calculus of my personal position was getting way too complex. Things would have been much simpler had I never found that thermos. For the moment, though, the number one priority was to prevent Delilah from being indicted, or to get her off if she was. That didn't require that I identify the killer, if in fact one even existed, nor did I need to prove anyone else was guilty. I knew that would be a practical impossibility. I just needed a scapegoat onto whom we could cast enough suspicion as to create legitimate doubt about who had done what. My number one candidate for the role was Marcelo Aguilar.

Marcelo had a beautiful young wife, whom he was known to treasure above all other possessions. Frank was responsible for helping her leave him, taking with her a considerable amount of cash in the bargain. Marcelo was famously hot-headed and was seriously pissed off about the situation and had publicly threatened Frank's life. So he was really pretty much a perfect fit. It would be a stretch explaining how he could possibly have spiked Capella's coffee thermos, but what the hell. With a good defense attorney that would be a detail easily finessed or glossed over. It was all about reasonable doubt, after all.

So after I said goodbye to Manny I headed to Coto de Caza, where Marcelo lived and where he'd agreed to receive me.

Coto is a high-end master planned community that lies in the Santa Margarita Valley along the inland western foothills of the Santa Ana Mountains, at the eastern edge of the county. The long drive from Costa Mesa gave me a chance to organize my thoughts concerning the approach I would take with Aguilar, the Porsche electronic box sitting in my trunk, and of course my poor Del. I had to wonder how long she could keep it together.

Once I reached my destination and drove through its very lovely neighborhoods and ascended its levels I could tell that the wealth and prestige of its residents was a sort of hierarchy defined by how high up the hill said residents dwelled. Sort of like monkeys in the jungle, you might say, with the biggest and smartest ones sitting in the highest branches. The homes got bigger and more elaborate along with the elevation.

The Aguilar estate was located at the very summit. An attendant checked my ID and waved me through a massive pair of wrought-iron gates and onto a winding cobblestone drive through a large terraced grove of avocado and olive trees, which eventually led to a traffic circle centered on an ornate fountain. It was only after emerging from the trees that the residence itself came into view. It was an impressive edifice, a three story block-out-the-sun Mediterranean piece of architecture that was the biggest private home I'd ever seen. I parked my car and walked up the front steps and rang the bell.

A maid pulled open one of a pair of massive mahogany doors and welcomed me in. She ushered me up one of a set of two mirror-image curved marble staircases that flanked the entry hall, to a second floor study where Marcelo was waiting for me.

As he stood to greet me I spread my arms and said, "Nice digs."

He laughed and said, "Thank you. We are comfortable here."

"I can imagine. Anyway, I'm sorry. Where are my manners? I'm Patrick Brennan, with Pacific Life Insurance."

"Of course. I know who you are, and I know why you are here, Mr. Brennan. I also know that you have other loyalties than to your position with Pacific Life."

Well, that was certainly unexpected. Apparently Mr. Aguilar is better informed than I suspected.

He's a squared off bull of a man, solidly built and though small in stature he has a commanding presence. His eyes and facial expressions have an intensity that mark him as a serious man, a very serious man. He's dressed simply in a white long-sleeved shirt open at the collar, blue jeans and a pair of cowboy boots. His skin is weathered in the way of those who have worked outdoors much of their lives. Despite the fact that English is his second language he speaks fluently and with little accent.

His study is lined on two sides with cherry bookcases filled with books and various memorabilia. Matched cherry pedestals display a pair of bronze statues depicting caballeros astride prancing horses. The far wall, behind his desk, displays dozens of framed photographs of himself posing with prominent people, along with a selection of aerials of his residential developments. It's bisected by a pair of French doors opening to a balcony.

He said, "I see that you are surprised. Don't be. I have many friends. Some of them like to gossip."

"I see."

"And so a man whose life I have publicly threatened is killed in a tragic accident. Then it is found to be possibly not an accident but a homicide. Your job becomes to investigate. But then you find yourself falling in love with a woman who has become the prime suspect..."

He raised his hand toward me and said, "No need to defend yourself. It is normal for a man to love a beautiful woman. I find no blame in that. And it is understandable and proper in these circumstances to wish to investigate other possible suspects. I'm not offended by that, and in fact I'm surprised that the authorities have not already beaten you to it."

I said, "Then you don't deny threatening Francis Capella's life?"

"Absolutely not. In fact I would consider myself dishonored if I had not. He took from me what I held most dear. And he made of me a *cabron*." As he said this he made the two-fingered goat horn gesture with his outreached hand, indicating he'd been cuckholded by Frank.

Without asking he stepped to the side bar and poured me and himself a couple fingers each of Patron *reposada*. He said, "Why don't we step outside, Mr. Brennan, and enjoy the view and this wonderful spring day? I think it may be helpful for you to hear a story I have to tell, an immigrant's story."

I said, "Fine. And you can call me Patrick."

He said, "Very well, Patrick. And you can call me Mr. Aguilar."

I smiled and followed him outside. We sat down at a small stone-topped table and for a few moments sipped tequila and enjoyed the view in silence. I waited for him to make the first move.

Finally he spoke. "You see, Patrick, I come from a family of peasants. Peasant farmers, I mean. I grew up on the outskirts of a small village in the jungle between Guadalajara and Puerto Vallarta in the state of Jalisco.

Villa Purificacion. Where we lived, out in the country, we had electricity, but only sometimes. We had no running water, but we lived near a small river, where we bathed, did our laundry and drew our drinking water. My people grew maize, yams, and beans. We had a couple of mango trees. We also had a few head of dairy cattle.

"As children our favorite treat growing up was a sweet concoction made of cow's milk straight from the teat, mixed with tequila and shaved chocolate. It was one of our very few indulgences.

"We were simple people and we lived a simple life, is my point. It's funny, but sometimes I think I may have been happier there than I've ever been since, despite my success and my wealth. I don't know."

He paused at this point and seemed to be lost in his thoughts for a long while. I chose not to interrupt his reflections.

At length he continued his soliloquy. "When I was sixteen my parents decided to send me to the El Norte, to the US. I have an uncle who lived in Santa Ana then, and they sent me to be with him. I crossed the border hidden in the tank of a cement mixer truck, Patrick, if you can believe that. Seems ages ago now.

"My uncle, Uncle Eduardo, worked in construction and so I went to work beside him. At first I was just an errand boy, fetching tools or carrying loads of materials, you understand. But I was always a hard worker and eager to learn and so I began to learn the trades of the men on our crew. At first I learned carpentry. I learned to drive nails, I learned to operate the power tools, I learned framing and roofing and hanging wallboard. Then I began to hang out with the plumbing crew and learned their trade. Then the painters, and finally the electricians. After a year, I could perform any task on a construction site, and perform it well. I became respected for my skills and started to make some decent money.

"My uncle and the men he worked with spent their time and money after hours drinking and chasing women. I didn't. I saved every penny and spent my evenings in night school at the community college there in Santa Ana, studying English. I knew from the beginning that would be the path to success for me.

"It took me several years, but eventually I had enough money to buy a small rental house. Since I was illegal my uncle arranged the financing and took title in his name. It was in bad shape, and I spent a lot of time getting it fit to rent, but when I did it was beautiful and the rent I was able to charge made all my efforts worthwhile.

"After a while I bought another house, and another, leveraging my rental income as I went. After five years I was able to sell out and purchase an entire apartment complex, always in partnership with Eduardo.

"Then I purchased a lot and built a house on spec. Soon came a bigger tract of land and several houses. In time I was a real player in the developer community. Eventually I became what I am today, the biggest real estate developer in the county and probably the state.

"Despite all my success though, I was still a rough-around-the-edges Mexican immigrant, not ready for polite society. And so I set about remaking myself. I hired a personal tutor to teach me to speak proper English and to eliminate my Spanish accent. I hired an immigration attorney to get myself documented. I enrolled in citizenship classes and became an honest to God American citizen.

"I can tell you, Patrick, that I love this country with all my heart. Of course I love my little home village and I love Mexico, but only in this country could I have achieved what I have. In honor of the United States I applied to the court to change my surname to Aguilar, which in Spanish means 'home of the eagle,' and I named my company Eagle Homes."

At this point he fell silent again. I said, "Well that's an amazing and impressive tale, Mr. Aguilar." He didn't respond.

Without comment he returned to his study and refreshed our tequila. We then both sat in silence for perhaps ten minutes, enjoying the splendid views afforded by his perch on the mountainside. The Santa Margarita Valley lay immediately below us, and to the west we could see the entirety of Southern California and the Pacific Ocean beyond. It was early evening by now, and the last of the sun was sinking into the water beneath a reddened sky.

Eventually he resumed his story. "Next I set about becoming a certified member of the club, the top level of Orange County society. I became a philanthropist and supporter of the arts. I threw fancy parties and began to be invited to everybody else's in return. I donated the land for a new Catholic high school, Santa Margarita High, and chaired the fundraising committee to get it built. I personally paid for the construction of the first building, Marcelo Aguilar Hall.

"So as I found myself approaching forty years of age, I had it all. Almost, that is. I realized there was one big thing missing in my life."

"A woman."

"Precisely, Patrick. For all those years of building my business, I'd denied myself the pleasure of a serious relationship. In my entire life I'd never experienced the love and companionship of a good woman."

I said, "So what did you do?"

"In answer to that I will tell you the rest of my story now, the most important part. I neglected to mention earlier that Purificacion has a well-deserved reputation for producing some of the most beautiful women in all of Mexico. The village was originally settled by the Spanish conquistadores, and to this day much of their blood flows through our veins. I believe it's that mixture of Castilian and Indian DNA that is responsible.

"That's where I found my Angelina. She first caught my eye on one of my regular visits home. She was the loveliest creature I'd ever laid eyes on. She was only thirteen when I first noticed her, but you could easily see that she would be a gorgeous young woman. On my next visit a year later I spoke briefly with her, just casual conversation. She was extremely shy and seemed unaware of her beauty. When she turned fifteen, I attended her *fiesta de quinceañera*, and presented her with a very expensive necklace. I also gifted her family with a large sum of money.

"Before leaving, I presented her parents with a proposition. I told them I wanted to bring Angelina to live with me in America, with the intention of eventually making her my wife. I promised them that she would not be touched until such time as we were married, certainly not before her eighteenth birthday, and that they would be able to send a chaperon to accompany her to ensure that my promise would be kept.

"I assured them that I meant no disrespect and did not intend that my wealth be used to coerce their daughter. I would spend time with Angelina under their supervision to give her the opportunity to get to know me and explain my plans to her and if and only if she voluntarily agreed would we proceed."

I said, "Which she obviously did."

"Yes, she did, as did her parents. We spent a week visiting and Angelina came to really like me. I don't know, maybe it was the necklace; young girls are so easy to charm.

"Anyway, I took her and her aunt, who would act as chaperon, with me when I drove back through the mountains to Puerto Vallarta. I called my attorney and had him pull some strings so that there would be no issues with immigration and green cards would be waiting for them both. We stayed at the Four Seasons in Punta Mita until that was accomplished and then I chartered us a private jet back to Orange County Airport."

I said, "So how did Angelina like America?"

"She was overwhelmed at first by the sheer scale and wealth of it all. Mind you she had never been outside of our village. I remember the first time I took her to South Coast Plaza. My God the excitement in her eyes! One thing all young girls, I suppose older girls as well, one thing they all love is shopping, and my Angelina took to that like a fish to water.

"And we were getting along well. Of course I respected my pledge and so our relationship was a platonic one. More like father and daughter, I realize, now that I look back on it.

"Those three years before we married were consumed with the project of preparing her for what would be her new life. I brought in my old tutor to teach her and her aunt English. Neither spoke a word of it when they arrived.

"I bought her a beautiful wardrobe and arranged regular visits to the best hair salons. I bought her jewelry and laptops and a cell phone, all the accessories an Orange County teenager requires to survive.

"One thing about these village girls, they do not have the benefit of proper oral hygiene, and so I arranged for the best cosmetic dentist in the county to correct that one and only flaw in her appearance.

"She was a princess, Patrick, a beautiful princess…a fairy tale come true."

I said, "Sounds like the story of Pygmalion come true to me."

"Ah yes. *My Fair Lady*. You are right, of course. She was my…what was her name?"

"Eliza Doolittle."

"Yes, thank you, my Eliza Doolittle. And so by the time her eighteenth birthday arrived she was a fully Americanized, fully formed vision of loveliness. Too Americanized, actually, as I eventually found out."

I said, "And then you married."

"Yes. The wedding was on her birthday. Of course it was a splendid affair, with hundreds of guests, the social event of the year. Cost me a fortune. Angelina was simply stunning in her gown, the most gorgeous bride ever to walk down the aisle. That night was the best of my life, and that's all I will say about that."

"I can imagine. And married life was good?"

"For years it was wonderful. We traveled, we threw parties, we made love, and we enjoyed all that life has to offer when money is no object. She learned to drive, and I bought her a convertible sports car. She became more independent and gradually acquired a nice circle of girlfriends. All spoiled little girls like her, of course."

I said, "So when did it start to go south?"

"As she grew older she just started drifting away from me. It was a subtle thing, so gradual I failed to notice until it was too late. It was my fault. All those years of building my business, I'd become accustomed to long hours and I understand now I paid too much attention to work and too little to her.

"I'm also a man accustomed to being in control and giving orders, and I guess she began to resent always being told what to do, how to dress and how to behave in public. I see now that because of the circumstances I had become both her husband and her father, and more and more she experienced me as the latter. 'I feel like I have no freedom to be myself,' she said to me at the end, 'and it's suffocating me.'

"I think as time went on the difference in our ages became a problem for her, also. Anyway, I swore I would change, that I would allow her all the independence she needed to be happy. But by the time I woke up it was maybe too late. She was complaining to her friends, and one of them gave her Mr. Capella's phone number. If there was any chance of saving my marriage, that son-of-a-bitch ended it. He convinced her that divorce was her best option. He turned my poor Angelina's head, and then he seduced her."

"Do you know that for a fact?"

"I know it in my heart. I asked her if she'd been unfaithful and she swore she hadn't. But I could see the truth in her eyes."

"All right. In light of that I have to ask you straight up. Did you have anything to do with Frank Capella's death?"

"I'm not a murderer, Patrick. I'm a religious man. I would not throw my soul away for revenge against this man. He was not worth it. My Angelina is gone, and nothing I can do will return her to me."

I had to admit, I was impressed with his sincerity. That didn't change the fact, though, that he was looking absolutely perfect for the role of alternative suspect.

At this point Marcelo stood and asked me to follow him. He led me back through his study and onto the walk way beyond, which was cantilevered along the inside perimeter of the second story rooms. The lower two levels of his humble little *casa* were constructed in an atrium style, so as we walked we had a view of the ground floor below.

As we reached the rear of the house we came to the master bedroom suite, which was enormous. On either side of the room were separate his and her bath and dressing rooms. The back wall consisted of a full width set of French doors that gave access to a balcony, which afforded a view of the pool area, pool house and tennis courts below.

He led me to what had obviously been Mrs. Aguilar's nightstand, on the far side of a massive colonial style canopy bed. There were only two objects lying atop it: a picture of Angelina, luminous in her wedding gown and a necklace, which he handed to me. It was a very simple piece, an elegantly fashioned gold chain pendant with a single stone, a heart-shaped pink diamond. I'm not GIA certified, but I can tell you that it was at least two carats. Genuine pink diamonds are many more times valuable than the colorless variety, and I could easily imagine that despite its unpretentious appearance I was looking at six figures. God knows he really did love this girl.

He said, "This was my gift to her for her *quinceañera*. I had it commissioned especially for her. More than anything it symbolized my feelings for her. It was the heart of our relationship. When we parted she gave it back to me. She said, 'Marcelo, you will find another little dove to love you. When you do, give this to her. And do not make her live in a cage.'

"That was a sad day, my friend, the saddest of my life."

His eyes were watering as he recounted her words and I found myself feeling sympathy for the man. I said, "Mr. Aguilar I thank you for your time and for sharing your story with me. I'm sorry that it didn't have a happy ending. Such is life, I guess. I hope that someday Angelina's words will turn out to be prophetic, and you will find another love. Not my place to give advice, but it's sometimes wise not to let the best be the enemy of the good. With that I will be on my way. It's been an interesting afternoon and again I thank you. Will you walk me out?"

As we prepared to part, standing at the entryway, a thought occurred to me. A conversation with his ex-wife might be interesting. I said, "By the way, where did Angelina go, then, if you don't mind my asking?"

He said, "She moved back to Mexico. She purchased a home in Punta Mita, near Puerto Vallarta. After all was said and done, she missed Purificacion and wanted to be closer. The village is a just a few hours inland from the coast."

I said, "I see. Well, adios then, Mr. Aguilar."

"Adios, Patrick."

On the way back to Costa Mesa I began to seriously weigh the possibility of a visit to speak with Angelina herself. Partly it was curiosity, but I also thought that she may give me a little more insight into Marcelo's personality and perhaps an anecdote or two that Delilah's attorney might find helpful.

Amazingly enough I was still on Pacific Life's dime, despite Del's arrest, and so an all-expense paid trip to Mexico didn't sound too bad.

CHAPTER 22

ABI TANAKA

When I returned home to Costa Mesa the message light on my answering machine was blinking. It was Mai. She said, "Hello, Patrick Brennan. It looks like you may be getting another chance to play house with your little girlfriend."

I've known Mai for a long time and when she uses my full name it's a sure sign she's unhappy with me. I also thought I detected a hint of jealousy in her tone, which I freely admit did not displease me.

When I rang her back I said, "So, Mingee. What's up?"

She said, "What's up, Patrick, is that our friend Abi is very conflicted at the moment. He's having a hard time pulling the trigger on your playmate. He can be such a woman."

Well, this was interesting. I said, "What's his problem?"

"His problem is that she was booked into the Newport PD holding facility at 11:30 yesterday morning. That means he needs to make a decision no later than that time tomorrow morning to charge her, or he has to release her."

"Right."

"The thing is, this is going to be a huge case. This is going to be the trial of the century for Orange County, and he can't afford to lose. He's looking to leverage his perfect record to move on to bigger things. Word around the campfire is that visions of Mrs. Tanaka and himself ensconced in the governor's mansion dance in his head. So he can't go forward until he is absolutely certain of a conviction."

"I see."

"Do you? Well that's a relief. You're maybe smarter than you look."

"Come on, Mai. This is too serious to make it personal."

"Sorry. You're right. So Abi was counting on turning Brad Johnson. Unfortunately we've been over the Club Neon tapes again and again and we don't see any exchange between him and Delilah, for instance a package containing GHB. Abi feels like he needs Longboard's help, and he was sure he could cut a deal with him. Obviously Brad is in deep shit. Very, very deep shit. He could easily be looking at a permanent change of address with the charges he's facing. But so far he's supporting Mrs. Capella's story."

Well, that was a surprise to me. A pleasant surprise, that is. Who would ever have figured Brad for a stand-up guy?

Mai said, "His attorney is making noises about the search warrant that led to the discovery of the tapes being invalid. I guess my beloved associates at the sheriff's office screwed up a few details on the paperwork. No surprise there. And with our recent record he might get some traction on that. Many of the judges around here are finished with cutting us slack. So maybe Brad's playing a waiting game. We will see. Meantime we have serious vacillation in the PA's office."

I said, "Well, Officer Nguyen, that's a goddamn shame. As you know I always come down on the side of our boys and girls in blue."

"Jesus, Patrick."

"Call me Pat, Mingee."

"Jesus, Pat."

"Okay, I'm sorry. Sometimes I can't help myself."

"Don't I know it? So anyway we'll see what happens tomorrow. And don't put the champagne on ice and turn on the mood music just yet."

"Right."

"Bye."

When I hung up I allowed myself the luxury of hope. Maybe Tanaka would blink. Maybe Brad Johnson would stay the course. Maybe the tapes would be thrown out. I began to imagine various scenarios of how Delilah's return home might go. What would that be like? Would she be so traumatized by the whole experience that we couldn't enjoy our reunion?

I ran out to the liquor store and picked up a bottle of Dom, just in case. Then I stopped by a florist and purchased a large bouquet of roses. Pleasant thoughts of the two of us enjoying time together again swam into my head. I won't kid you. Most were X-rated.

Unfortunately, it was not to be. At precisely 11:00 AM the next morning the grand jury returned an indictment against Delilah for first degree murder.

I couldn't do anything about it or speak with Delilah for the rest of the day, so I decided to drive down to UC Irvine and visit Dr. Scott again.

I found him in his office, grading test papers.

He said, "Good morning, Patrick. You've been a busy boy, I hear. Seems you're a minor celebrity."

"Uh, yeah I guess so."

"Not my business, but do you think it's wise getting involved with that woman? Doesn't look to me like there's much of a future there."

"We'll just have to see, Doc. Time will tell. Anyway, I have a hypothetical question for you."

"Shoot."

"After I spoke with you last time I paid a visit to the Porsche dealership. The manager gave me a tour and let me inspect a car that was very similar to Capella's. We discussed the computer chip that controls the engine."

Dr. Scott said, "Right, that's become pretty standard practice in the industry."

"Well this guy seemed very proud of it. He made it sound like it was a really special piece of work."

"He would, wouldn't he?"

"Hah, yes I suppose he would."

"So what do you want to know?"

"What if that chip just stopped working for some reason? Wouldn't that have the same effect as lifting off the throttle? Couldn't that have been the cause of the accident, in theory?"

"Hypothetically, yes, I suppose so. But Patrick you are really grasping at straws here to help your girlfriend. The chance of a chip like that just spontaneously failing is vanishingly small. I've never heard of it happening. These chips all have a built-in safe mode they revert to in case of a problem."

"Yes, so I was told. But what if there was some sort of electrical shock, like maybe a voltage spike, or a short circuit or something like that?"

"I don't know, Patrick. But it matters little. The chip in that car could not possibly have survived the crash. There'd be no way to examine it forensically."

I decided not to mention my visit to Manny and the impound facility. I just said, "I guess you're right about that. Thanks, Doc."

"Be careful with Mrs. Capella, Patrick. You're playing a dangerous game. You don't want to get dragged into her mess. There are a ton of women out there for you."

"The heart wants what the heart wants, Doc."

"I'm pretty sure it's not your heart that's driving the train, my friend."

"Hah. You may have a point. I won't deny that she's great in the sack. It's always hard to tell where lust ends and love begins."

"That's the problem with us men, unfortunately. Anyway, just be careful. Whether it's love or lust don't let it get you into trouble you can't get out of."

CHAPTER 23

DELILAH

Hope is the cruelest of all human emotions, and nowhere has that sad fact been written more clearly than on the face of Delilah Capella as I smile a half-hearted smile at her across the thick piece of glass between us. We each hold telephone hand pieces to our ears. She is a mess, her face streaked with tears and her shoulders visibly shaking.

She said, "I made a big mistake, Pat. I allowed myself to get my hopes up."

I said, "I understand, Del, trust me. But truth be told, it would only have been a temporary reprieve. They're not going to give up on this, they can't. You should read the papers. This case is blowing up all over the media. They're having a field day and it's mostly at your expense. The 'Newport Black Widow,' they're calling you."

"His kids had a memorial service for Frank. Maybe you heard. They sailed his boat out of the harbor with a bunch of his friends and spread his ashes into the open sea. They held a news conference when they returned and aimed some very unhelpful remarks in your direction. Big frigging show."

"I haven't been watching the news, obviously, but sure, I can imagine. They want to make damn sure they collect the insurance money."

"Bingo. Judging from the accident photos Mai has shown me, they didn't have to spend any money on cremation services, by the way. Anyway, the prosecutor is coming down hard on Brad Johnson to say the magic words. They still think they can flip him but so far he's sticking with your story. I have to say I would never have expected that."

"I guess he has a decent heart after all, in spite of his sins."

"Yeah, well maybe. But it's a real worry, especially if the search warrant is upheld and his tapes are ruled admissible. I mean, he's looking at life. They'll have huge leverage they can use to turn him. How's that going to match up against any friendship he may feel for you?"

"I don't know, Pat. I don't know I don't know I don't know. Maybe he has a conscience."

Where was his conscience when he was drugging and raping underage girls, is what I was thinking, but I didn't have the heart to voice my thoughts. I could see that Del was just mentally defeated. I decided to change the topic. I said, "So I had a visit with our friend Senor Aguilar yesterday."

She said, "Thank you, Pat. What do you think?"

"Hard to say, Del. He was seriously pissed off at losing his young bride, that's a fact. He freely admitted that he was angry enough to kill Frank, and that he publicly threatened to do just that. He's convinced that Frank was sleeping with his Angela.

"But then he claims he had a change of heart and realized revenge wasn't worth it. Any way you slice it he's our best candidate though, no doubt about that. He had motive. The opportunity bit is difficult, I'll admit. I've been thinking about that, and it occurs to me that he could have used a honey trap."

"What?"

"A honey trap. A woman. Say just for grins, he seriously decides to take out your husband. How do you attack any man? You use his weakness against him. What was Frank's weakness? Women, of course. So he hires a beautiful woman to meet the poor bastard and reel him in. Aguilar has friends everywhere. He can know when and where Frank is at any given time, and he can orchestrate the whole scenario.

"So maybe he's out catting around one night in a bar, where this woman approaches him. She puts him under the ether. They begin a relationship. Just saying, now, go with me here.

"What comes next? The night before your husband's death, she texts him. She can't stop thinking about him, she needs to be with him, she says. Let's meet down the hill at the Starbucks and we can have a quick roll at one of the many lovely hotels in Laguna, she says. He meets her, she begs off the sex but takes the opportunity to spike his thermos, either at the coffee shop or maybe they slip into his car to exchange a brief farewell kiss and she does it then."

"I don't know, Pat. That's pretty far-fetched. I don't think there would have been time for him to do that. I have a real problem believing it."

"Okay, so maybe the plan all along was just for a quick meet to arrange a later tryst. Work with me, darlin'. It matters not what you can or cannot believe. We are trying here to create reasonable doubt in the mind of one juror. Understand?"

"Yes. Okay, I see."

"Good. There's one other thing. I think I want to pay a visit to Angelina. Marcelo told me she's in Puerto Vallarta."

"Why, Pat?"

"I just think it might be helpful to get her take on the divorce and how everything went down. Maybe she'll have something helpful to say about the state of Marcelo's mind. Maybe she would even be willing to testify to Marcelo's intent to kill your husband. Can't hurt, might help, and I'm still on Pac Life's dime.

"Meantime, we need to get you some decent representation. You're not talking to the detectives or prosecutors, right?"

"No. They've assigned a public defender to me since I have no money. She seems to really want to help, but she's, like, just a kid right out of law school. I need a lot better, Pat, but where is the money coming from? All my friends were friends of Frank first. It was his social circle we moved in. His group wants to see me convicted. They all think I'm guilty. They're not breaking out any cash. I'm praying for a miracle, Pat. That's what it's come to."

"We both are, Del. Believe me, we both are."

CHAPTER 24
JT 'TEX' HOLLIDAY

Amazingly enough, Delilah's prayers were answered two days later when a black Gulfstream IV touched down at John Wayne Orange County Airport and taxied up to the Atlantic Aviation private terminal. The lone passenger who emerged from the plane's passenger cabin and proceeded down the stairs and into Atlantic's VIP lounge was the celebrated JT "Tex" Holliday.

I'd heard about Mr. Holliday and was somewhat familiar with his reputation. He was currently one of the hottest defense attorneys in the country. He'd burst onto the scene when he was able to get an acquittal in the celebrated murder case of Robert Maddux. Maddux' wife had shot him to death, and the ensuing trial was every bit as big a media circus as Delilah's was looking to become.

Robert "Big Bobby" Maddux was a billionaire wildcatter who resided in Odessa, West Texas. Late in life Big Bobby had dumped his wife of over thirty years and taken up with one Miss Shyla Larieux, a buxom young lady one third his age whom he'd met in a Fort Worth gentleman's club. Eventually he made her his bride, and when his four children objected he disinherited them and changed his will to leave everything to her.

Unfortunately, the fairytale romance came to a violent end one evening when during a drunken argument Shyla pumped six .357 rounds into him from a Colt King Python revolver.

There was no question that Shyla had killed him and her chances at trial were looking pretty dismal. Self-defense was going to be a tough sell after she squeezed off the third or fourth round. With your .357, one is generally sufficient.

So along came JT, a colorful sort who always wore a Stetson ten gallon hat, fringed leather jacket and Lucchese boots, and who fancied himself a born again Texas cowboy. He actually claimed to be a descendant of Doc Holliday, the famous gunslinger. In reality he'd grown up in Brooklyn, only recently drifted into Texas, and could not tell the ass end of a horse from the front. But what the hell, why let the truth get in the way of a good story?

Fortunately for Shyla, JT had an amazing connection with juries and mounted a brilliant defense. He basically resorted to a stratagem that could only be appreciated in Texas: the bastard-had-it-coming defense. Big Bobby was a famously offensive character, a man given to bullying, cheating in business and lying. It was said he was the kind of man that would climb a tree to lie when he could stand on the ground and tell the truth.

JT argued that Maddux had abused Shyla, though no evidence ever emerged to support that allegation, and that he'd been a serial adulterer, a charge he was able to back up with a string of Bobby's ex-mistresses.

The highlight of the trial occurred when Shyla, who opted to testify, was being cross-examined.

At one point the prosecutor asked, "Now Mrs. Maddux, you shot your husband with a .357 Magnum revolver. That's a hell of a weapon for a little woman such as yourself, isn't it?"

Shylay answered, "I suppose so, sir. But then I'm a hell of a little woman."

"So you may be. But why did you shoot six times?"

"The gun only held six rounds, sir."

The fact that the jury had to struggle to suppress their laughter at her answer may have been a clue as to which way the wind was blowing, but going into jury deliberation the prosecutors appeared to be very confident. Long story short, the jury was out just a few hours before returning a not guilty verdict. The shocked look on the face of the two prosecutors was exceeded only by the expressions on the faces of the four disenfranchised Maddux siblings.

Holliday made his bones with that case, and never had to buy lunch or advertise his services again in the great state of Texas. Soon well-heeled defendants from all over the USA were reaching out for his services.

You had to give it to him. He had a real genius for theater. His advance team had arranged a news conference and reporters were awaiting his arrival. Upon entering the VIP lounge he strode straight to the microphone.

He said, "Ladies and Gentlemen, I've come to offer my services to Delilah Capella. I am certain that this poor woman could not have murdered her husband. This is the weakest circumstantial case I've ever seen. There is exactly zero real evidence linking her to what was most likely an unfortunate accident. Let me say it again: she is 100% innocent. She is the victim of an abusive, overreaching prosecution at the hands of a notoriously ambitious prosecutor. I have a limousine waiting outside and I intend to drive straight to the Santa Ana Women's Detention Facility and speak with her. If she will have me, I will defend her at trial, pro bono. I'll have more to say later. Thank you."

CHAPTER 25

JT AND THE MEDIA

The next morning JT Holliday called another press conference. He'd lost the leather fringed jacket and cowboy boots. For this occasion he wore a custom-tailored business suit, silk tie and Italian loafers.

He still sported the Stetson, but laid it aside before he spoke. He said, "Good morning. I'm happy to report that I spent a few hours with Delilah Capella yesterday and she has graciously accepted my offer to defend her. I will tell you that any fool who actually spends time with her will realize that she is completely incapable of murder. She is a delightful young woman, a gentle Christian woman, a minister's daughter for God's sake, with not a shred of malice in her heart.

"The case against her is a circumstantial one, and in fact the only germane circumstance here is the fact that she was married to the victim. Yes, she had opportunity. So did many others. That's where it begins and ends. She had no motive, while there are many who did. As you well know, Mr. Capella had more than his share of enemies.

"This has been a disgraceful rush to judgement by the prosecutor. I cannot say that the investigation by the OC Sheriff was a shoddy one, but that is only because there *was* no investigation. I will later today be filing a motion with the court for a summary judgement for dismissal. There simply is no case here.

"Now if you will permit me I need to address some remarks to you, the members of the press and broadcast media. You have all been grossly unfair to my client. You have portrayed her as some sort of *femme fatale*, which she obviously is not. This is the worst sort of journalism. It is irresponsible. I understand that you need to sell papers and you need your TV and radio ratings, but please remember that in this country guilty until proven otherwise is still the law. Do not put this woman on public trial with your lurid reportage. Leave the trial to the courts. Give her a break. That said, I will be pleased to take your questions. Please state your affiliation before posing them."

Here is a brief recap of how the Q and A went:

"Thomas McCain. CBS affiliate Channel 8 TV: Mr. Holliday, you say that your client had no motive. But what about the money? Aren't we entitled to follow the money? Her husband was a very wealthy man, after all."

"Well sir, that's a fair question. Forgive me, but that's an issue I prefer to address at trial."

"Lloyd Thomas. KOCR AM. Frank Capella was a well-known player when it came to the ladies. Isn't it possible that his wife wanted him dead because of his infidelities?"

"Delilah was of course aware of the rumors. But she loved her husband dearly and he loved her. The two were working hard on their marriage at the time of his death. As I've mentioned, my client was a God-fearing lady, and for her forgiveness was a religious duty. As a matter of fact they had marital relations the night before Frank died."

"James McCook. Orange County Register. Do you believe the house-keeper had a part in it?"

"I have no reason to believe so. I can't imagine what her motive may have been. But then, unlike Mr. Tanaka and his single-minded focus on my client, we are ruling no possibility out."

"Monica Woodson. OC Weekly. Are you worried that Brad Johnson will testify against your client?"

"Not in the slightest. He has nothing to which to testify, except that Delilah is innocent and there was no drug exchange between them. She met him at Club Neon only as an old acquaintance she was trying to help. The club video confirms that."

The conference ended on a drop-the-mike moment for Holliday when someone shouted out, "Tanaka is claiming his case is iron clad."

JT answered, "Well sir, Mr. Tanaka can claim that his pig is a racehorse, but that doesn't mean it's going to win the Kentucky Derby."

With that he walked out of the room to a round of laughter.

CHAPTER 26
THE HONEY TRAP THEORY

After the presser JT spent the rest of the day filing motions with the court, reading witness statements and studying the pretrial disclosure material provided by the PA.

First thing the next morning he called me and asked that I attend a conference he was scheduling with Delilah for that afternoon. He wanted to give her a status report and briefly outline his game plan for her defense. We'd had occasion to talk a couple of times and I'd filled him in on what my investigation had turned up, and in view of that and my relationship with Del he thought it appropriate that I sit in.

I headed up to Santa Ana, to the detention facility, right after lunch. I arrived half an hour early, but JT was already there, waiting. He had an associate with him, a big scary looking bald guy dressed all in black whom he called Pete, and who only nodded when we were introduced. I'm not sure to this day if Pete possesses the power of speech.

Tex said, "Pete is my handyman, Patrick. He wraps up all the loose ends for me."

I wasn't sure what sort of loose ends Tex needed wrapping up, but at any rate Pete reached into his briefcase and pulled out some sort of electronic gizmo with which he proceeded to scan the room.

"Bugs, Patrick. Just checking. You can't be too careful with this bunch."

Shortly thereafter Delilah arrived and Pete left. He didn't favor us with a good-bye or me with a "nice to meet you."

They brought her to the conference room in handcuffs, the bastards, which they removed only after she was seated. She looked pale and haggard, and appeared to have lost maybe ten pounds she didn't have to lose. She didn't make a pretty picture, I can tell you for nothing.

She said, "Hi Patrick. God it's good to see you." She reached across the table and gave my hand a quick squeeze. She managed a brave little smile.

"Hello, baby. Yes, it's great to see you too. How you holding up?"

"I'm okay. Mr. Holliday has been a godsend. He's kept me going and given me hope. I don't know what I would have done without him."

Holliday said, "Okay, so here's where we are. Yesterday I filed a motion for dismissal. Unfortunately it was my motion that was dismissed this morning, not the indictment. That's fine, I expected it. It was just a pro forma exercise, the sort of thing we lawyers do.

"I also filed a motion for a change of venue due to the prejudicial pretrial coverage the case has received. It's pending but will probably be denied as well. Good news is that if things go south on us that will be an excellent cause for appeal. But don't worry, things aren't going to go south."

I said, "Well, that's a relief."

"You bet, partner. Now, there is one more item to brief you on before we get down to business. You may have heard the old adage that trials are won and lost at jury selection. I can assure you that that is the God's honest truth. Just to let you know, I have my associates running focus groups of the various demographics we'll be considering during the *voir dire* and selection process."

I asked, "Any clarity so far on what type of juror you'll be looking for?"

"Some. My gut tells me young women and old men are the ticket. The women her age will identify with Delilah, and the men will fall in love with our little lady here, I'm thinking. We'll see. But that's a call I'll make, so no need to concern yourselves with it."

After a few moments of silence he continued, "The real reason I have you both here is to fill you in on the broad outlines of my strategy for our defense. I think it will be a real confidence builder for you both. Unfortunately the good old 'bastard had it coming' approach is not going to fly this time. That dog will hunt in Texas; not so much in California.

"My overall approach has always been to construct a series of defensive layers, or firewalls if you like, to deflect the prosecutor's attacks. Each layer has one and only one purpose: to create reasonable doubt in the minds of jurors. To get a conviction the prosecution is going to have to drag twelve jurors through each one of them, dispelling all shadow of doubt at every step along the way. The idea is that the prosecution might be able to pierce one or more of them, but never all of them. If I've done my job well, the end product will be a structure that Tanaka and his crew will never be able to overcome."

I said, "I sure hope you're right JT. As you know, I have my sources. They tell me Tanaka is running around telling anyone who will listen that this case is a mortal lock."

"Well, I've noticed that our friend Abi has a tendency to say giddy-up to his mouth before his brain's engaged. That will not serve him well at trial, I promise you. Pride goeth before the fall, right Mrs. Capella?"

Del summoned up another weak smile and nodded her Biblical confirmation.

"All right then, here we go. Our first layer of defense is the most obvious, that this is an entirely circumstantial case. And as I told our friends in the media, the only real, solid circumstance that ties Delilah to this death is the fact that she is married to the decedent. Hell, we don't even know that this was not a simple accident. There is furthermore no evidence to prove that this poor woman spiked her husband's coffee. Think about it…if she had done so why would she have volunteered to the police that she'd been the one to prepare his thermos? They could never have proven that on their own.

"We don't know where Frank went or what he did after he left the house. We don't even know that he actually drank from the thermos before he died, no one does. Due to the condition of his body there was no autopsy so it cannot be proven that there was actually GHB in his system. As a matter of fact the witness statement given by Mr. Fenner indicates that Frank was navigating that winding road successfully for some time, and doing so with his foot solidly planted into the pedal. That sound like someone who's been drugged?

"For me it is just as likely if not more so that he laced that coffee himself. Let's face it, the man could not keep his dick in his pants to save his life, sorry Delilah, so maybe he had a date set up and the GHB was intended to guarantee a happy ending.

"Bottom line is there's nothing dispositive here. Absolutely nothing.

"Now, second up is the fact that there has been an irresponsible rush to judgement in this case. A rush to judgement that this was a murder rather than a simple tragic accident. A rush to judgement that if it was in fact a homicide, the only possible perpetrator was our lady here. A rush to judgment that nobody else on God's green earth could possibly have been responsible for Frank's death. This was despite the well-known fact that Frank had a ton of enemies.

"The sad reality is that Mr. Brennan here has done a thousand times more of an investigation than the staff of the Orange County Sheriff's Office, who have basically sat on their fat asses for weeks and done fuck all, sorry again Delilah, by way of actually doing their job.

"Have they bothered to interview any of the defendants whom your husband creamed in court lately and are known to be highly pissed off at him? No. Have they interviewed any of the women whom he represented and may still be seeing? No. Have they pulled video from any of the many establishments along Frank's intended path to see what he may have been up to? No.

"What they *have* found the time to do is give self-serving interviews, they and Tanaka as well, talking about what geniuses they all are and how they have Delilah dead to rights. It's pure 100% bullshit and I will drive that fact home with the jury, drive it hard, and if that ain't a fact God's a possum."

At this point JT paused and came up for air. He was really worked up. I could see that once he was on a roll he could really take a jury for a ride. There was no wonder he had the reputation he enjoyed. I began to feel very good about Del's chances. I thought to myself that this trial may actually turn out to be fun. He'd even sucked Del into his world. She was sitting there wordlessly, her eyes as big as quarters and an enigmatic little Mona Lisa half smile blossoming on her face.

After a few moments he continued, "Now the third layer, and a personal favorite of mine, is the friend of defense lawyers everywhere, the good old *ad misericardiam* ploy, the shameless appeal to pity. Here this poor little innocent girl from Iowa, a naïve minister's daughter, moves to the big city hoping to make something special of herself. She inadvertently falls in with a sketchy crowd, including most notably our friend Brad Johnson.

She extricates herself from that bad situation and falls under the influence of a much older, powerful man, with whom she falls in love and marries.

"This man provides her a very luxurious life style, and as far as we know really does love her. But his children and associates mark her as a gold digger and treat her disrespectfully. She learns the hard way that beneath the veneer of surf and sunshine Newport can be a very tough town.

"To make matters worse, she is publically humiliated by the philandering of a faithless husband. But she bravely soldiers on. She is herself a loyal wife, a devout Christian wife, and she tries as best she can to make her marriage work. Against all odds her husband responds to her efforts. They seek counseling and are well on the path to a solid reconciliation.

"It's precisely at this point that fate intervenes and she suffers the tragic loss of her husband. But that is not enough, no. She barely has time to begin grieving before an overly ambitious prosecutor brands her as a murderer and in the blink of an eye, with no legitimate investigation or legal process, she finds herself indicted for a crime she is utterly incapable of committing.

"Yet the slings and arrows keep flying. She is crucified in the press as a gold digging *femme fatale*. The 'Black Widow,' the headlines scream out. She is imprisoned and driven to a state of despair, near total mental collapse."

JT paused for a moment, and then said, "I promise I will have tears in the eyes of all twelve of them, the jurors. I will paint for them a verbal picture that will break their hearts. Delilah, I'm 99% sure I'm going to put you on the stand. It's a risk worth taking, I think. You have an aura about you that is just so genuine and open and vulnerable. I saw it the minute I met you and I knew immediately that you were innocent. I want the jury to see that first hand. They will not be able to resist you."

Delilah said, "My God, Mr. Holliday. I don't know if I can do it. I'm going to be terrified just even sitting there in court, I know I will."

"Don't you worry, sweetpea. It'll be easier than you think. All you have to do is be honest, as you have been all along. There's no 'story' that you have to keep straight. You have nothing to hide so they won't be able to catch you out on cross. Just tell the truth. The truth will set you free."

She nodded and said, "Okay then. I will try."

"Trust me darlin', you'll do a damn sight better than try. And so now we move into the heart of the line up, so to speak. The three layers I've mentioned so far are all generic, the sort of garden variety defenses that Tanaka will anticipate and be prepared to counter. But the next four are all out-of-the-box arguments. If the other side's investigation has been as sloppy as I believe, we will totally blindside them.

"There is first the matter of motive. It takes two things to make someone a suspect: opportunity and motive. Opportunity is your one and only real weakness, Delilah, because no one in Orange County had as perfect an opportunity to spike Frank's coffee as you. So we need to eliminate motive. Fortunately, Patrick has directed my attention to the details of your financial arrangements with your husband, to wit your prenuptial agreement, which calls any ostensible motive seriously into question.

"Let's make sure I understand correctly. I'm given to believe that you were only seven months away from a five year milestone in your marriage, Delilah, at which point you were to receive one million dollars, cash. Is that correct?"

Delilah said, "Yes, that's correct."

"And you were only five short years and seven months from being granted a full share of your husband's estate, and the prenup would effectively be extinguished at that point, is that correct?"

"Also correct."

"And you have that in writing?"

"Of course. Notarized and on file with the attorney who drew it up for us."

"Well, I can tell you it's going to be a thing of beauty when that little piece of information comes out at trial. Who the hell would take the risk of committing murder when they can hang in for a few lousy months, collect a million dollars, and ride off into the sunset if they wish? Or tough it out for a few more years and really break the bank?"

I said, "Exactly. You hit the nail on the head. I mean, there *is* the insurance money but is the risk worth the extra bucks? Not to mention Delilah's a beautiful young woman who if she divorces would be a hot property on the market. She already had Frank's associates salivating over her, and she wasn't even trying. You know she's going to remarry well. It doesn't make sense."

JT said, "I do believe the jury will agree with you, partner. And so now we move on to our next layer, which is the existence of alternative, plausible suspects for our jury to consider. It will be impossible for them to return a guilty verdict if they can be convinced there are others out there who could reasonably have been responsible. Here again, your investigation has been extremely helpful, Patrick, and I agree with you that our friend Mr. Aguilar will make a perfect poster child for the effort. Who the hell knows if he was actually involved but that's beside the point; he sure could have been. He was demonstrably out of his mind with anger at Frank, and he's admitted to threatening his life. I'm going to put him on our witness list and ask to have him subpoenaed. It should be really entertaining to have him on the stand and play around with him a bit on direct. I'm not sure the court will approve, and Abi's certain to object, but we'll try.

"Then there's the housekeeper, Lourdes. She had opportunity, but the motive's a little tricky. It's possible someone paid her. Actually, it's convenient for us that she's disappeared, most likely back to Mexico. I can suggest that she fled because she had something to hide, and she won't be around to defend herself. She would probably be a sympathetic witness if she actually appeared, so we'll keep our fingers crossed she doesn't pop up. Anyway, we'll throw her in the mix."

I said, "I've been considering going down to Mexico myself. That's where Aguilar's ex-wife, Frank's client, is living. She may be able to give us some little nugget of information that would be helpful. I'm really curious to get her take, and the insurance company is still picking up the tab."

JT said, "Good idea. Yes, please do that."

I said, "Okay, I'll get a ticket, probably leave in the next couple of days."

"Perfect. Just don't drink too much tequila down there. That shit will give you a wicked hangover."

"Sounds like the voice of experience, Tex. I'll bear it in mind."

JT said, "And now on to our next surprise, for which I'm indebted once more to you, Patrick, the 'honey trap' theory. Patrick tells me you and he have already discussed it, Delilah. I love it, and I plan to go with it.

"The biggest problem we face, as I see it, is trying to give the jury a plausible manner by which the GHB could have been introduced into Frank's thermos *after* he left home.

"The honey trap is our perfect answer. Let's say one of Mr. Capella's many enemies, for example just to pick a name out of the hat, Mr. Marcel Aguilar, wants to do away with him using the very novel and damn near foolproof method of drugging him while he is driving a fast and famously unstable automobile.

"How can this be done? Well, how about the time honored strategy of using Mr. Capella's weakness for women against him? Say Mr. Aguilar recruits a lovely lady to ensnare his victim? Mr. Aguilar is extremely well-connected throughout the county. It would be child's play for him to determine an appropriate time and place for her to make her approach. Say she hooks up with him in a bar one night. They initiate a hot little affair. Say that on the fateful Saturday morning she asks him to meet her at the Starbucks down the hill from his house, so that they can arrange a tryst for later in the day. She's sipping a cappuccino when he arrives, but he of course has his own coffee, which he brings with him. Or they decide to take a quick trip around the block in his car while they talk, with his thermos sitting in the cup holder between them. Either way she distracts his attention, drops the mickey into his coffee, they hug and kiss good-bye and with a seductive little wink she's on her merry way.

"Patrick, you are a goddamn genius. The beauty of this argument is, first, that it's impossible to disprove it didn't happen, especially when no camera footage was pulled from along Frank's route, and second it expands the field of possible suspects from three to dozens. Any of Frank's enemies could have done it this way."

At this point Delilah was once again sitting across the table wide-eyed and wordless.

I said, "Thank you, JT. It is a fact I cannot deny. I am one creative and devious son-of-a-bitch."

He said, "Hah. Indeed you are."

"Now the last line of defense is going to be the most fun of all. My researcher back in Austin was doing a media search and came across the Orange County Register series of articles that ran two years ago exposing corruption in the Sheriff's Department. It's a pretty ugly picture: planted evidence, bogus lab results, coerced confessions, mysterious inmate deaths in the Santa Ana detention facility. Promises were made at the time and much lip service was paid to reform, but as far as we can tell no substantial changes were ever made.

"I'm going to call the Sheriff himself to the stand. He won't come willingly, I'm sure, so I'll have to drag his ass into court with a subpoena. What's that clown's name, Reyes? When I'm done examining him no one in that court is going to trust his department to give them the time of day, let alone be willing to send a woman to prison for life based on his department's evidence.

"When I get through with him Sheriff Reyes will be working night shift security at some second-rate strip mall."

CHAPTER 27
LONGBOARD

For all of Mr. Holliday's bravado we all knew that Brad Johnson's long shadow still hung over Delilah's fate. If the PA could get Brad to throw her under the bus she was finished. So far he was hanging tough, but Mai assured me he was getting worked over hard. I decided it would be good for me to have a conversation with him face to face to see how he was doing. If he was getting wobbly we needed to know.

Early the next morning I reached out to Mai and asked her to contact him and ask if he'd see me. I still had a couple of days to kill before heading to Puerto Vallarta and so I wanted to get to him as soon as possible. She came back to me later in the day with the news that he was anxious to speak with me, and I headed back up to Santa Ana.

When they brought him into the visitor's room I was struck by his change in appearance. Unlike Delilah, incarceration was actually agreeing with him. He looked nothing like the gaunt long-haired surfer I was used to seeing in the papers, his face drawn and aging. In the press photos it appeared that his lifestyle was catching up with him. But now he'd packed on a few pounds and appeared much healthier. The jailhouse haircut had done away with his golden locks but the tan had yet to fade.

I started to introduce myself and explain why I wanted to see him when he held a hand up and said, "I know who you are, Mr. Brennan. I've been following Del's case in the Weekly and read all about you and your relationship with her. I'm glad you're here. I've wanted to somehow get in contact with Del and reassure her that I would never lie about her to help myself. She's a great girl, a real straight shooter, and I could never do that to her. I don't know if she killed her husband or not, but I'm okay with it if she did. The bastard had it coming as far as I can tell. But she didn't get any GHB from me, and I'm not testifying otherwise."

I said, "Well Brad that's good to hear. I appreciate your candor. They're putting a ton of pressure on you, I hear."

"Oh yeah, you can't believe it. They're offering me two choices. Door A I swear I gave Del the GHB and they give me the keys to the city, throw a parade, name a day for me and forget all about that nasty date rape thing. Maybe I plead out and get a couple years plus probation. Door B I stick to my story and they lock me up and throw away the key."

I said, "Jesus, they really want her bad."

"No shit. I guess she's a much bigger trophy for Tanaka to put on his mantel than some low-life rapist. Go figure."

"Yeah, go figure. So you're in some really deep trouble and if you don't cooperate they will come at you with everything they've got."

"Yeah, that's the size of it. There *are* a few rays of hope, though. My attorney discovered that they screwed up the search warrant, the dopes, and he may get the videotapes ruled inadmissible. I'd still have some issues, but nothing like what those tapes would do to me. Why the hell I made them, I'll never know. Oh, and they never taped me being Mirandized so any dumb ass thing I may have said when they interrogated me, before I wised up and asked for counsel, is scratched. But I'm not kidding myself; I could be looking at life. I'm not sure how I could handle that. But don't worry. I'm not bailing on your girl. I have enough bad karma as it is, enough for two lifetimes."

I said, "And so, I have to say, you're looking pretty good. Much better than your newspaper pics."

"Yeah, you know it's funny but getting thrown into jail may have been a good thing for me. I've had a real epiphany since I've been off the drugs and the booze and the partying. It's given me real clarity on what a fucked up asshole I've been. Looking back on it now, I can't believe the shit I did. It's unreal, like a bad dream.

"I haven't always been Longboard, you know. Actually I was a real nerd in high school. I was a straight A student. I used to read a lot. I always loved literature. It was only because I could surf like a son-of-a-bitch that I got to hang with the cool kids. I was captain of our team, you know. We were state champs all four years. That's a big deal in Newport."

I said, "I can imagine."

114

"My dream was to go to UCLA and study film. I was going to be a great screenwriter. I could have gotten in, too, but my family couldn't afford it, even with in-state tuition. So I went to Orange Coast, the community college, instead. That's when I went off the rails. I made the wrong friends. I can tell you, once you go down the drug rabbit hole it's hard to climb back out."

"Were you there when Delilah was a student?"

"Yeah, I used to see her around some. We didn't hang out. She had too much sense to get involved with my crowd."

I was beginning to sympathize with the poor guy. I said, "Well, I hope things work out for you, Brad. I'll be sure to tell Delilah what you said. You're a real stand-up guy. Hang in there. Is there anything I can do for you?"

"Now that you mention it, with all this time on my hands I'd like to start reading again. I could sure use a book. One of the classics, maybe."

"Sure. Who would you like? Faulkner? Steinbeck? Hemingway? Fitzgerald?"

"No, not twentieth century American. I've read all that. I'm thinking something older, English maybe."

"How about Dickens?"

"There you go, that's the ticket. Get me a copy of *A Tale of Two Cities*. That's a nice dark one, from what I know of it. That's very appropriate to my present circumstances."

"You got it. Good luck to you, Brad."

"Thanks, Mr. Brennan. And thanks for the visit."

"My pleasure, and you can call me Patrick."

"Thanks, Patrick."

When I returned home I ran down an online publisher that produced hard bound copies of all the great books. I ordered a nice leather-bound version of Dickens' classic masterpiece for Longboard and had it delivered to the detention facility.

Next I phoned JT at the makeshift office he'd set up at Newport Center and gave him the welcome news that he could breathe easy.

115

CHAPTER 28
ANGELINA

Puerto Vallarta has always been my favorite Mexican City. It's ideally situated on Bahia de Las Banderas, the Bay of Flags, at the northwest corner of the state of Jalisco, famous as the birthing waters of the Pacific Humpback whale. There's always a cool onshore breeze and the city is far enough north that it doesn't suffer the stifling heat that afflicts cities further down the Pacific Coast. It still retains an old world Mexico charm, the food is wonderful, the locals are friendly and it's largely escaped all the unpleasantness of the drug wars.

At the northern end of the bay, across the border in the neighboring state of Nayarit, is Punta Mita, a peninsula dedicated entirely to perhaps the most luxurious resort in the entire country of Mexico, featuring Four Seasons and St. Regis hotels, golf courses, beach clubs and multimillion dollar villas. This is where Angelina is living, and this is where I was headed.

The three hour flight from LAX passes over the border at Tijuana and then cuts diagonally across the Baja peninsula and the Sea of Cortez to Mazatlán. From there we proceeded south, skirting the coastline. To our left lay the coastal plateau, which consists of desert scape punctuated by farmland and framed by the background of the Sierra Madre Occidental mountain range; to our right the vast expanse of the Pacific. As we neared our destination the mountains grew closer, the plateau narrowed, and the landscape shaded greener with jungle vegetation.

My flight arrived in the afternoon, and by the time I cleared customs it was too late to drive up to the resort. I thought it better to present myself at Angelina's doorstep in the morning, in the daylight, rather than in the darkness of night when she may hesitate to open her door for a stranger. I would have loved to spend a few extra days in the city, maybe enjoy an authentic Mexican meal in the old city, stroll along the seawall, the *malecon,* or head south along the coast to the beaches of Mismaloya. Unfortunately, CalLife was adamant about limiting me to two days, and two days only. So I needed to see Angelina first thing in the morning, do my interview, and get back to the airport for my flight home. I rented a jeep at the airport and drove out to the marina and checked into a hotel.

When I rolled up to the guardhouse at Punta Mita's entrance the next morning I handed the attendant my PI license and a couple of hundred-dollar bills while asking in my high school Spanish for directions to Mrs. Aguilar's villa. He proved to be very cooperative; he marked Angelina's *casa* on a map of the property and handed it to me.

Her villa is a two story structure with very clean modern lines, flat-troweled earth tone stucco and burnt sienna tile roof, beautifully landscaped with tall coco palms, bougainvillea and native flowering shrubbery. I pulled onto the cobblestone driveway, stepped out and walked to the front door.

I'd been told, of course, that Angelina was beautiful, but when she opened the door I realized that was an understatement. She is stunning. Her eyes are an iridescent deep green. Her hair is the color of sable and glows in the morning sunlight; it flows in straight tresses nearly to her waist. She is indeed a little angel.

She is dressed in a simple black jumpsuit that complements her hair. She cradles a Siamese cat in her left arm, which she strokes with her right as we speak. She's a petite young woman, and her height and slight figure remind me of Delilah. It's striking to me that these two young women, so alike, should be linked by the sad circumstances of Frank's death.

I showed her my license, my ID and a couple of clippings from the OC Register that featured photos of me due to my connection with Del. I explained to her why I was there and why I wished to speak with her.

She said, "How did you find me, and how did you get into the resort, Mr. Brennan?"

"Well, your ex told me you were living here, and the gentleman at the gate seemed to think I was okay, especially after I showed him a couple portraits of Ben Franklin."

She laughed. "Oh yes, of course. Welcome to Mexico, home of the *mordida.* And you've spoken to Marcelo, then, have you?"

"Yes. My job basically at this point is to look at anyone who may have had a motive for killing Mr. Capella. As you know your ex-husband was a little put out with him."

She laughed again. "Yes, just a little put out. All right then, come in. I was just having a light *desayuno*. Perhaps you'll join me."

She padded barefoot across the limestone living room floor, which was completely open to sweeping views of the Pacific by virtue of sliding glass panels, and led me onto the stone pool deck beyond. She invited me to join her at a low table covered with plates of mango, breakfast pastries, a bottle of San Pellegrino sparkling water and a pot of black coffee. Kitty took up residence in her lap.

She said, "You must try the mango. It's right off the tree."

I said, "Really. Do you grow your own?"

"No. Unfortunately mangos don't love the ocean air. These are from a plantation in the interior. I have them delivered."

She was right. The mangos were amazing. I said, "This is a truly splendid residence, Mrs. Aguilar. Right out of Architectural Digest. How did you happen to land here?"

"Marcelo had me stay here, at the Four Seasons, while he was arranging US entry papers for me."

"Oh yeah. He mentioned that to me."

"As you can imagine, I fell in love with it. It's the most beautiful spot on earth, and the community is extremely private and extremely safe. Or at least I thought so until you showed up at my door. Also it's close enough to Purificacion for me to make frequent visits."

After a few more moments of making small talk while I busily stuffed mango and *pan dulce* down my throat she asked, "So what exactly did you come here to ask me, Mr. Brennan? And by the way, as far as Frank's death is concerned, I thought that his wife did it."

I said, "We're not sure about that. There have been some complications. Anyway, I guess I would just like to know about your marriage to Marcelo. I'm trying to gauge what sort of man he is. I visited him and had a brief conversation with him, but you are obviously much better qualified to judge."

"Where would you like me to start?"

"At the beginning, if you would. I'd like to follow along the full arc of your relationship with your ex-husband."

She said, "Well, all right. Here goes. As you know I'm a peasant girl, born into a family of peasants living in a town of peasants. I don't say that to disparage my background. I'm quite proud of it. These are good, honest, hard-working people I'm talking about. I just want you to appreciate what a, how do I say it, a disorienting experience it was to arrive in America. As you Americans like to say, it blew my mind. It's as if I'd landed on a different planet. It was exhilarating and terrifying at the same time, if you can imagine."

I said, "Of course. And Marcelo treated you well?"

"Oh yes. He treated me wonderfully. He was always respectful of the arrangement he'd made with me and my parents. He showered me with presents and gave me the best education money could buy. I was living a life of unimaginable luxury. It was a fairytale come true."

"And so in time, you married. The very day of your eighteenth birthday, I understand. Did that change things at all? Did he treat you differently after that?"

"No, not really, except of course that we were now sharing a bed."

"Forgive me for asking, and you don't have to answer, but did you enjoy that aspect of your relationship?"

"Well, you really are a nosy man aren't you? That's all right, I don't mind. It might even be...how do you say...?"

"Therapeutic?"

"Yes, that's it. Anyway, sex of course was completely new to me. I'd never so much as kissed a boy before the night of our wedding. But Marcelo was a patient lover and I gradually came to enjoy it, yes."

"But the marriage eventually failed. Why was that?"

"It was a combination of several things, really. Marcelo never mistreated me or abused me in any way. I was always his princess. But as I matured his treatment never adapted to the grown-up me. He was by nature a very controlling man. I guess you don't get to his level of success without being like that. He just could never let me spread my wings, even just a little bit. In the end he was just suffocating me."

"The little bird in the gilded cage, people have said."

119

"Exactly."

"So, forgive me again for putting you on the spot, but Marcelo told me he was certain that you slept with Mr. Capella once the divorce was in progress. Mrs. Capella believes that to be the case, although Frank never admitted it to her. What is the truth, if may ask?"

She gave me an odd little smile and said, "What would you like my answer to be, Mr. Brennan?"

"I guess I'm good either way. Just the truth will do."

"Frank and I never had sex. He was always a perfect gentleman."

"I see."

"However, I *was* unfaithful to Marcelo, actually, before I filed for divorce. My husband could always read me. When he confronted me with his suspicions I tried to lie but he could see it in my eyes. He just assumed that it was Frank."

"I see again. And who was the lucky gentleman?"

"It doesn't matter. It was one of Marcelo's foremen. It was brief, meaningless and not even enjoyable. I was just trying to assert some independence I guess. It was stupid."

I said, "Well then, tell me this. Overall, do you believe that your ex is the sort of man that could have been involved in Mr. Capella's death?"

"I doubt that very much. Marcelo is a devout Catholic. I cannot believe that he would ever have put his immortal soul in danger. I also believe that toward the end he came to see that the divorce was partly his fault, and some of the anger softened."

"Okay, thanks."

"Anyway, how could he possibly have done it? Frank was drugged, right?"

"I was thinking that perhaps he got to the housekeeper."

"Lourdes? There is no way she was involved."

"You know her?"

"Do I know her? She's my aunt. She was my chaperon that accompanied me when I moved into Marcelo's house."

Well, that came as a real shock to me. The sound I was hearing was the sound of another piece of the puzzle falling into place.

Angelina said, "Naturally, when I left Marcelo she had to move out as well. Frank agreed to hire her as his housekeeper as a favor to me. She had no love for Marcelo I can assure you, and no reason to help him."

I said, "How about money?"

"She doesn't care about money. And anyway, I have more than enough to provide for her needs. Of course, she could see that after Frank's death she might come under suspicion. That's why she fled back here, to Mexico. She visited me, in fact, for a few days. She swore she did nothing to the coffee."

"And so you know where she is?"

"Of course. So do you if you're any kind of investigator and can put two and two together. But she won't talk to you and she will never return to the US, if that's what you're hoping."

"No. I'm fine with her right where she is."

With that I stood up to leave and said, "I really do want to thank you, Mrs. Aguilar. You've been a real sport. I mean, some crazy American man shows up unannounced on your doorstep and wants to pry into your personal life. Not many women would have rolled with that."

She said, "Well, to tell you the truth I always welcome an opportunity to have a conversation in English. I want to keep my proficiency up. And I like American men, crazy and otherwise. But you might call ahead next time."

I'm not positive but I think I caught a quick wink there as she said that.

She then said, "You know, there was a moment, when I first opened the door. I was afraid you were DEA."

I said, "DEA? Why would you think that?"

"Frank's wife didn't tell you about the drugs?"

"Uh, no. What drugs?"

She said, "Sit back down, Mr. Brennan, please, and I'll explain. I probably should not reveal what I'm about to, but for some reason I trust you. You must swear that what I say goes no further. Will you do that?"

"No problem. You have my word."

"Back during the financial crisis Marcelo came close to bankruptcy. He was desperate for cash. He was way overextended. He'd been on a building spree because things were going so well, and suddenly he had all this inventory that wasn't selling.

"One day one of his guys came to him and offered to put him in touch with drug traffickers based here in Puerto Vallarta. Marcelo has a large yacht, over a hundred feet. Too large for Newport so he keeps it in San

Diego. He commissioned it after we got married and christened it *Little Angel,* but since the divorce he's probably renamed it.

"We used to sail to Puerto Vallarta occasionally, and Marcelo's reputation around the harbor was impeccable, so the idea was that he could bring a load of cocaine every time he returned and customs would never suspect him or search his ship. It turned out to be a good idea, because he was able to bring in several huge loads successfully and bail himself out of financial trouble.

"Of course he never told me what he was up to, but I accidentally overheard a conversation about it."

I said, "Seriously? That's unbelievable So what did you do?"

"I confronted him. I told him he was crazy. The *narcotrafficantes* are not people you want as playmates. If a deal gets crossed up bad things are going to happen. And issues with the criminal justice system are going to be the least of those bad things. But by this time he was hooked on the easy money and told me to stay out of it.

"Things were already sort of coming apart for us anyway, but this is what really pushed me over the edge and made me file for divorce. I was not interested in being indicted as a co-conspirator in a federal drug smuggling case and I sure as hell was even less interested in having my severed head end up in a UPS package on overnight delivery back to Coto de Caza, attention Marcelo Aguilar, signature required."

I said, "Yeah, I can see where that would have been the smart move for you."

"Anyway, once I filed for divorce I told Frank about it. Naturally he used that information to leverage a much better settlement out of my husband. To this day I'm still not sure whether Marcelo was angrier over getting squeezed that way or over his suspicion that Frank was screwing me."

I said, "You've sure given me a lot to think about, Mrs. Aguilar. I'm going to be on my way now and again thanks so much for your help."

As I reached the door she touched me on my shoulder and gently pulled me around to face her. She said, "Tell me. This woman you are trying to help, this Delilah. Do you love her?"

I found that to be a very interesting question, one to which the answer needed to be carefully parsed. I decided on, "I'm pretty sweet on her, you could say."

"And you believe she's innocent?"

"I'm certain of it."

"Well, you tell her I will be praying for her, please, that God will grant her justice. I know something about being in her position. A young girl married to a powerful man, I mean. There were also those who whispered behind my back."

On the flight back to LA that evening there were three things running through my head. First was the lovely and well-heeled Mrs. Aguilar. Was that remark about liking American men just a throwaway line, or was there something more? Had she left a door open to me?

Then there was the Lourdes situation. That was definitely manna from heaven for JT and I couldn't wait to tell him. I was being honest when I told Angelina that I was happy with Lourdes being sequestered in Purificacion. She was much more helpful to us there than on a stand in an Orange County courtroom.

As for the drug thing, I decided I wouldn't mention that to JT. I figured I would squirrel that little nugget away for a rainy day.

CHAPTER 29
LONGBOARD R.I.P.

It was a couple of days after I returned from Puerto Vallarta. The radio woke me up and I heard people talking about the death of Brad Johnson. I listened for a few minutes but became frustrated that no details were being given, so I picked up the phone and called Mai.

Right away she said, "Morning Patrick. I was going to call but I was waiting for a little later. Didn't want to interrupt your beauty sleep, you know."

"So what the hell, Mingee?"

"The hell is that Mr. Johnson hung himself in his cell sometime between bed check last night and wakeup call this morning. Yesterday a judge ruled the search they conducted of his apartment legal, and his videotape collection admissible. His choices after that were pretty stark: roll over on Mrs. Capella or spend at least the better part of his remaining life in a cell."

"Jesus Christ, I can't believe it. Is there anything your department can't screw up?"

"That's a real popular question right now. I tell you it's a real shitstorm. Over at the PA's office my contact tells me Brad's attorney is screwed through the ceiling. She's a PD, you know. Brad had no money; he pretty much lived life on the pay-as-you-go plan. Anyway, she's making a lot of noise about resigning from the county, going into private practice and representing the family in a very large wrongful death lawsuit."

I said, "So I guess Sheriff Reyes is really thrilled about this."

"Sheriff Reyes is set to have a news conference at 10:00 AM. I promise you he isn't looking forward to it. He's going to get crucified."

"I'm sure. That's the one piece of good news you have for me."

"Well, there's also the fact that this breaks really, really well for your girlfriend."

"You're right about that. Holliday will have a field day with this. The narrative writes itself. Poor Longboard is subjected to relentless pressure

124

from the prosecutor to lie about Delilah and finally breaks down mentally. And the hopelessly incompetent Sheriff's Department fails to prevent him from harming himself, despite the fact he was an obvious candidate for suicide watch. Oh yeah, it's gonna be a real party."

Mai said, "If you'll permit me to interrupt your gloating, I need to tell you that Brad left you something. A book was found in his cell. There was a note scribbled on the front page. He basically apologized to the women he'd victimized. He said he couldn't bring himself to give false testimony and he couldn't face life in prison. At the end he wrote that he wanted the book to be returned to you. If you like I can run it down to your place at lunchtime."

"I'd appreciate that. I'll grill us some burgers."

"Okay, see you then."

When she handed me the book and I read the note, I just knew somehow that Brad had more to say. Something told me to flip over to the last page and I saw that my intuition was right. Underlined was the final passage of Dickens' novel, the farewell statement of his protagonist before being guillotined:

"It is a far, far better thing that I do than I have ever done. It is a far, far better rest I go to than I have ever known."

Cynical bastard that I am, I had to admit that I was well and truly touched. I thought to myself, God speed, Longboard, God speed. I hope surf is up wherever you are. You were a better man than we knew.

CHAPTER 30
PRETRIAL

Three days before the trial was set to begin JT set up one last pretrial conference for Del and me. His ostensible purpose was to bring us both up to date on all the recent developments, but I was pretty sure he really just wanted to shore up Delilah's state of mind. She was very fragile at this point and she really needed to hold it together, particularly if she would be taking the stand.

Once we were all assembled he said, "I just wanted to let you know that I'm feeling extremely good heading into trial. Our motion for a change of venue has been denied, which was a big mistake on the part of the judge and would get her reversed in a heartbeat on appeal but it doesn't matter because we are going to win this thing outright anyway. I can also tell you that I'm pretty happy with our preparation for jury selection. My team has done a great job with the focus groups, and I know just what I'm going to be looking for.

"I'll be brutally honest. Mr. Johnson's demise, tragic as it was, is a godsend of a game changer for us. When this trial begins, there will now be three people, actually, on trial. One will be Sheriff George Reyes and his corrupt, incompetent department. Of course the prosecutors will see this one coming and be ready to do whatever damage control they can. Good luck to them with that.

"Next up will be our friend Mr. Aguilar. Thanks to Patrick's efforts, we have another game changer, the connection between Lourdes and Aguilar. This is one the other side will not see coming, because I will not reveal the fact that Lourdes was the aunt of Mr. Aguilar's wife and had lived as his guest for years until the testimony phase of the trial. I can't wait to hear Mr. Tanaka whine that we didn't share that information with him earlier, and point out to the jury that this is a perfect example of the poor police work done by the OC Sheriff's investigators. Had any sort of real investigation been performed they could easily have uncovered this information for themselves. Instead they took the path of least resistance, a rush to judgement.

"And then finally, of course, we have Delilah. My intent is that at the end of the day she will in the minds of the jury be the least guilty of all the parties involved.

"I have another little Easter egg or two for Tanaka et al, but I'll get to that when the time is right."

At this point JT's phone rang and when he saw the caller ID he said, "Excuse me. I have to take this. It's my office."

He stepped into the hallway and was gone for 10 or 15 minutes, while Del and I held hands and pretty much just looked at each other without speaking.

When JT returned he said, "Well, I'll be damned. I didn't see this coming. There's been a development we need to discuss, Delilah. One of Tanaka's toadies called thirty minutes ago and spoke with one of my associates. They want to play let's-make-a-deal. They prefer not to go to trial. They're offering you a plea deal. You plead out to second degree murder and they'll guarantee a sentence no longer than ten years. You could be out in five."

Delilah was shocked, naturally. She said, "I can't plead guilty to something I didn't do."

"Don't get me wrong, Delilah. As your attorney it's my duty to advise you of the offer. After that the decision is up to you. Tanaka is obviously less confident than he was when he indicted you. The circumstances have changed dramatically. I could probably hold out for manslaughter, with an eight-year sentence. Maybe you do three or four. If we go to trial and lose you're looking at a minimum of twenty, and probably more."

"But I'd have to plead guilty. I'm not guilty, Mr. Holliday."

"I know you're not, of course, Delilah. Technically, you would not need to admit to any guilt. They said they'd agree to an Alford plea."

"A what?"

"An Alford plea. What you would basically be stipulating is that while you maintain your innocence, you recognize that the prosecution has enough evidence that they could win a conviction. It's a pretty common maneuver."

"Are you saying you recommend I do this?"

"Hell, no. But I have to present the option to you. It's your life and your freedom on the line. I'm very confident, and the fact that they're making this offer tells me they aren't. Unfortunately they're in too deep, though, to just drop the charges. They need to save face and arrange a graceful exit or just carry on."

"All right, then, let them carry on."

JT slammed his fist down on the table and said, "Excellent. So we go to trial. I'll tell them to shove their plea agreement."

I said, "I'm with you all the way on that."

JT said, "So now, Delilah, I'd like to address the question of your testimony. As I said, I lean toward putting you on the stand, if you're willing, but that' a decision we'll make down the line. We have plenty of time; if you do testify you'll be my last witness. Should we make that decision we'll make certain you're very well prepared. We'll practice your direct examination and you'll know every question I plan to ask you and be prepared to give an effective response. After that I'll have one of my most mean-spirited associates play the part of Abi and do a mock cross-examination with you."

Delilah said, "Thank you. That sounds fine."

"Good. So I'd like to take a few moments and sort of outline the way your testimony would go. I've made a preliminary list of questions I want to ask, and the sort of answer I want to hear. It's a work in progress right now. My main priority is preparing my opening statement, but at least it will give you the general idea so you can be thinking about it."

At this point I excused myself and left JT and Del to finish their conversation.

When I got home the first thing I did was put in a call to Mai. I was curious if she knew about the plea offer.

When she picked up I said, "Hey Mingee, can you talk?"

She said, "Not right now, and not here, but I'll get back to you on my cell once I'm out of the building. I think I know why you're calling."

She called back in an hour and when I picked up said, "You're calling about the plea offer, correct?"

"Yeah. Did you know about that?"

"Not officially, but we all saw it coming. Reyes has been putting a ton of pressure on the PA's office because he realizes a trial could ruin him. Word is the County Commissioners have also let it be known in no un-certain terms that they don't want a trial. There is no way OC comes out of it looking good, what with the old scandals that would be resurrected.

"Then finally, Tanaka himself is a whole lot less certain of his case than before, and going to trial with uncertainty is not his style. Remember, in the beginning he was thinking he'd be up against a public defender, not the most successful defense attorney in the country. Plus he figured he'd have Longboard in his hip pocket. It would be real convenient for him if he could get a win by default."

I said, "Well, he's going to be disappointed."

"Your girlfriend's not playing?"

"No. No way."

"Hmm. Very interesting. If nothing else this is going to be an extremely entertaining show."

"Oh yes, Mai, you've got that right. Very entertaining indeed."

CHAPTER 31
THE TRIAL: OPENING STATEMENTS

The day Delilah's trial began was the first hot day of the young summer. A massive high pressure system was parked off the coast of Baja and was spinning warm, moist air into Southern California. The Santa Ana civic plaza was sweltering, the air hot and sticky.

The media frenzy surrounding the event had reached a fever pitch. The story had gained national attention and network vans with their satellite antennae filled the street in the front of the courthouse. All the outlets had flown in their top on-air talent. The area swarmed with humanity, everybody trying hard to be part of the proceedings. The lucky few who actually secured seats in the courtroom had queued up on the courthouse steps overnight.

The general wisdom was mostly siding with the prosecution. A few offshore gambling sites were even taking action on the outcome, and Tanaka was going off as a three to two favorite.

Interestingly enough, the narrative's focus had shifted over the preceding week away from Delilah herself and onto the opposing attorneys. The press was having a field day with the prospect of JT and Abi squaring off against each other. They were calling it the battle of the undefeated heavyweights.

Many or maybe most in Orange County regarded Holliday as a showboating hillbilly who'd just blown in on a dusty Texas breeze, a man whose cheap theatrics would never fly with the sophisticated citizenry of California. But then, they didn't know JT like I did.

Speaking of JT, he himself was feeling very confident. Jury selection had wrapped up the day before, and he was generally pleased with the outcome. There were five women whose ages generally matched Del's, two of whom were divorcees. There were a couple of older men, one of whom was himself in a May-December marriage, a fact JT thought helpful. There were four jurors of Hispanic ethnicity, one African-American and the rest were Caucasian. Tanaka had pushed hard for the Hispanics; we assumed he guessed they might harbor very little sympathy for a rich little white girl. Abi of course had to get them all. We only needed one.

At this point, I feel I need to make an important point to my readers. Most of you, I am certain, have never attended an actual murder trial, much less served on a jury for one. If your only experience of courtroom proceedings comes from watching the ID channel you have no idea how excruciatingly ponderous said proceedings can be. This particular trial was destined to consume two and a half weeks. Therefore time and space do not permit me to provide a blow-by-blow recounting of the trial record. Rather, I intend to offer a summary recap of the opening and closing statements, and specific detailed highlights of witness examinations and cross-examinations that I believe most germane to the flow of battle, if you will, and most telling with regard to the final outcome.

I'd never seen Abi in person before, and I was surprised to see that he was much taller than I'd imagined. He was lean, his face thin and angular, his swept-back hair thick and jet black. He wore a tailored black suit, silk tie and expensive-looking dress shoes. The economy and precision of his movements about the courtroom, plus his overall bearing, made me wonder if he'd had military experience.

JT on the other hand wore a white shirt with western style trim and bolo tie, suede vest, khaki dress slacks and Lucchese boots. Out of respect for the court his Stetson was left parked on the table in front of him.

As is normal practice, the prosecution got first shot at the opening statements, and last at the closing. This is intended to afford a slight advantage to balance the fact that the state is burdened with proving its case beyond a reasonable doubt.

Abi Tanaka's speaking style was the polar opposite of Holliday's. It was dull and passionless. His words were spare, direct and lacked any trace of elegance or emotion. Nevertheless they were brutally effective, like a tack hammer slowly and relentlessly driving a ten-penny nail into a piece of hardwood. Not for nothing had he won every case he ever prosecuted.

The ancient Greeks had a saying that while the fox has many ideas, the hedgehog has one big idea. Abi played the hedgehog. His opening statement drove home one point, again and again, to the jury: while many may have had motive to harm Francis Capella, one person and one person only had opportunity, and she was sitting in the courtroom at the defendant's table.

He was well aware, of course, that the defense intended to cast suspicion elsewhere and he worked hard to preemptively attack that notion. He challenged the jury to try and imagine any possible manner, any conceivable manner on God's green Earth, by which they might imagine anyone but Delilah introducing a harmful substance into Frank's coffee thermos. Plainly written on the face of every juror was the fact that he had made his point and made it damn well: they couldn't.

When his turn came JT jumped right into what I can only describe as a virtuoso performance. Where Tanaka lacked passion, JT absolutely and whole-heartedly embraced it. He took immediate command of the courtroom, his words resounding with the fervor of a well-rehearsed preacher. And he *was* indeed preaching, preaching the gospel of Delilah's innocence. The jury hung on his every word as if in the throes of a religious experience.

There is an old rule of thumb about delivering effective sermons: tell them what you are going to tell them, then tell them what you have to tell them, then tell them what you told them. That's precisely what JT did.

One by one he cited each of the points of defense that he'd discussed with Del and me in pretrial conference: that this was a strictly circumstantial case with no direct evidence linking his client, that the state could not prove that Frank had actually ingested the drug-laced coffee or that the drug had not been introduced after he left the house, that the sheriff and prosecutors had rushed to judgement to the exclusion of all potential suspects other than Delilah, that in fact there was little to no monetary motive for Delilah to harm her husband, that she was a woman of unquestionable moral rectitude who was a good wife trying hard to make her marriage work, and finally that the sheriff's department, along with the PA's office, had a well-known, proven history of corruption that made it impossible for a reasonable jury to convict and send to prison his client on the strength of one small piece of evidence, the GHB.

He ended by promising the jury that each of these salient points would be backed up by witness testimony, that he was writing each of them a check that they would be cashing as the trial went forward.

He then pulled off a piece of theater that only he could have come up with. He'd reserved three seats in the front row of the spectator's gallery for members of his team. The three stood up and left the courtroom once everyone was called to order.

With much flourish JT pointed to the three empty seats and said, "Ladies and gentlemen, I promise you that there will be not one but four people on trial starting today. Those seats are for the other three. None of them are present, but they should be. The first belongs to Orange County Sheriff Reyes, whose inadequacies I intend to document very thoroughly. The second is for Mr. Marcelo Aguilar, a man famous for his violent temper and a man who publicly threatened the life of my client's husband. The third is for Lourdes Perez, the Capella's housekeeper, who had free access to Francis Capella's coffee thermos, who has conveniently disappeared and who is assumed to have fled the country."

Of course, Tanaka was absolutely apoplectic at this little stunt and immediately demanded that the judge strike Holliday's remarks. The judge, Theresa Russo, a woman known as a fair-minded judge but one who would not put up with any nonsense, chastised JT very harshly and ordered his words stricken from the record.

It mattered little, of course. The jury could not "unhear" them; the damage was done. It was an exquisite bit of showmanship. JT had fired the first shot across Abi's bow. He'd scored and everybody knew it. It was on.

CHAPTER 32

THE TRIAL: TESTIMONY

As important as the opening statements and closing arguments made by attorneys are, they are basically just hot air. It's the testimony of witnesses that establishes the facts upon which the jurors make their decision.

As I've mentioned, Abi Tanaka's case was a simple one, and his witness list reflected that fact. He called just five: Francis Capella's two children, the CSI technician who worked the accident scene, the county medical examiner and the senior sheriff's detective that led the investigation.

Frank's children were a couple of good-looking fresh-faced kids, early twenties, with SoCal tans and blonde hair they didn't get from their father. Sheryl Capella wore a knee-length summer dress and leather sandals, her brother Roger an expensive-looking cashmere blazer, white dress shirt open at the collar and designer jeans. They seemed, well, prosperous I guess is the word.

Sheryl painted a very unflattering picture of the marriage between Delilah and her father. She depicted Del as a gold-digging opportunist who seduced her father with her youth and beauty, in the process wrecking the relationship between her parents who, though separated, had been working on reconciliation. She complained that after the wedding Delilah had sought to exclude her and her brother from any contact with their dad, and banished them from the new couple's home. As I watched the jurors' faces I could see that she was having an impact. They looked displeased.

Surprisingly, JT declined to examine her on cross. I assume he judged that her brother's testimony would be a repetition of the same charges, and that it would be wiser to go after him rather than attack the young woman and make her even more sympathetic than she already was.

As expected, Roger Capella's testimony was a rehash of his sister's. When it was finished and his turn came, JT started out soft with his cross-examination. He said, "Mr. Capella, first of all I want to say that I'm very sorry for your loss. Your father's death was a great tragedy. But if you don't mind I'd like to ask you just a few questions."

Roger said, "All right."

"So, when your father married the defendant you and your sister would have been how old?"

"I was eighteen, my sister sixteen."

"I see. And when your parents separated, then you would have been eleven and thirteen, correct?"

"That's correct, yes."

"That's very young. It must have been hard for you. And I'm sure you both were very anxious to see your parents get back together. That's completely understandable. But wasn't that really just a fantasy, a child's wishful thinking with no real grounding in reality?"

"We believed it." He pointed a finger at Delilah and said, "And I still believe it would have happened if that woman hadn't come along and destroyed everything."

JT said, "Well, let me ask you this if I may. Had your father ever actually indicated that he was contemplating reconciliation with your mother?"

"Not explicitly, no."

"And did he ever tell you that he was dissatisfied with his new marriage? Did he ever suggest for example that the defendant was anything other than a good and loving wife?"

"No."

"And so he was happy in his marriage to the defendant?"

"I guess so."

"And then, did the defendant ever say to you that you were unwelcome in her home?"

"Not in so many words."

"Then would it not be fair to say that it was your anger with the situation that caused you and your sister to break off contact with your father, and not some scheme on the part of the defendant?"

Roger said, "It's a matter of interpretation, I suppose. We believed what we believed."

JT said, "Yes, a matter of interpretation, indeed."

At this point, he took off the gloves. He said, "Mr. Capella, your father was a wealthy man and his new wife was a relatively young woman. Did it occur to you that after the marriage your share of the estate, as well as your sister's, had just been reduced from one half to one third? And might it not have been this fact that caused you to choose, rather than celebrate your father's happiness, to shun both him and his wife?"

"It was never about the money."

"I'm sure of it. But speaking of money let me ask just one more question please. Do you know what happens to the proceeds of your father's life insurance policy should the defendant here be convicted?"

"I haven't a clue."

"Perhaps I can be helpful to you. Would it be a clue if I told you that my associate recently had a conversation with one Ms. Francine Gilliam, who is an executive with Pacific Life, the company that issued the policy, and who stated that she had spoken with you, that you had inquired concerning that very question and that she had informed you that in the event of a conviction the accidental death indemnity would no longer apply, but the face value, two and a half million dollars, would go to you and your sister? Would that jog your memory?"

The look on Roger's face was priceless. He squirmed around in his seat for a few moments and finally said, "I'm sorry. I guess I misspoke."

JT said, "I guess you did. You do realize that you are giving testimony under oath in a murder trial, do you not?"

"Yes. Of course. I'm sorry."

JT then pointed to Delilah and said, "And you do realize that this woman's life and liberty are at stake?"

Roger didn't answer.

JT said, "Mr. Capella, you and your sister have a huge financial stake in the outcome of this trial, millions of dollars, and you both know it. Would it be fair for the jury to conclude that your testimony today is compromised, and should be totally disregarded?"

Once again Roger failed to answer. He was probably too busy wondering why the hell he'd ever agreed to take the stand.

The testimony of the next two witnesses, the CSI tech and the ME, was fairly uneventful. The tech spun a lovely little yarn about finding Frank's thermos on the side of the hill above the smoldering remnants of his Porsche, and I was tempted to stand up and yell *you lying son-of-a-bitch, I found that thermos and there's no clean evidence chain,* but that would not have been in my best interest and anyway Del was going to get off regardless. JT declined to ask him any questions.

The ME could only testify to the obvious fact that the accident was not survivable. JT asked him on cross whether or not he'd found GHB in Frank's body, but he was only firing for effect. Everybody knew that Frank was incinerated.

The final prosecution witness, Michael McCormick, was the Sheriff's Department's senior detective. He wore a rumpled off-the-rack suit jacket over a wrinkled shirt, his hair was unkempt and his shoes were unpolished. The thing was, his reputation as a smart cop with great natural instincts and his seniority meant he didn't have to worry about appearances.

Abi led him through the details of his investigation, such as it was, in what was clearly a well-rehearsed exchange. While he was on the stand a short clip from the Club Neon video was played for the benefit of the jury. Delilah and Brad were clearly featured, of course, and it was sort of weird to see Longboard brought back to life. Detective McCormick provided the accompanying commentary.

After Abi finished with McCormick, JT sat motionless in his chair for a few moments, until Judge Russo finally said, "Mr. Holliday? Do you care to cross examine the witness?"

JT hesitated, as if trying to decide whether to do so or not, and finally said with a *what the hell shrug* of his shoulders, "Uh…yes your honor, I guess just a few quick questions."

I had to laugh. It was classic Holliday theater.

After he approached the witness stand he paused once more, as if composing his thoughts. He said, "That was a very nice video that you showed us, detective. I wonder, though, why you chose not to show the part where the GHB was exchanged?"

McCormick said, "We don't have it."

"Oh? You mean there are gaps in the tape?"

"No. They just weren't always on camera. There are spots in the club that aren't covered, like say the restrooms."

"So is it your theory that my client met with Mr. Johnson in the men's room, or do you figure he joined her in the ladies'?" This was the only moment of levity in the two and a half weeks of trial, but JT wasn't smiling. I could see something in his expression that told me we were about to be treated to the unveiling of one of his Easter eggs. McCormick was somehow walking into a trap.

He said, "I couldn't tell you. Maybe they have unisex restrooms."

JT said, "You mean you don't know?"

"No."

"You're telling us that you have never been to this club?"

"I have not."

"Then who was it that performed the investigation? Who mapped out the floor plan and camera coverage? Who interviewed the staff?"

"No one, to the best of my knowledge. We sent a patrol car around to pick up the videotape, and that's all we were interested in."

"Detective McCormick, can we agree that this videotape is a pivotal piece of evidence in this case? In fact so pivotal that the prosecutor declined to indict my client until it was discovered?"

"Yeah, I guess so."

"Yet the Sheriff's Office did not think to physically inspect the scene of its creation, to understand the context of what you were seeing?"

"No."

"Well, we did, actually. My team performed a thorough investigation of the club and interviewed the staff at length. I can tell you that the camera coverage is excellent. Anything and everything that happens in the public spaces there is captured. As for the restrooms, you may rest assured that they are gender specific. Moreover each has a full time attendant whose main job is to insure that they are not used for drug dealing of any kind. The club had developed a bad reputation in that regard and the owners were concerned for their license."

Detective McCormick was looking tired. He could only mumble a weak, "I see."

"So I think we can agree that not only are you unable to prove there was an exchange, but that such an exchange could hardly have occurred without detection, is that right?"

JT saw that Abi was standing to voice an objection and said, "Strike that last question. I will move on."

He then turned again to the detective and said, "Since we are on the subject of GHB, I do have another small question. It certainly looked for all the world that Mr. Capella's death was an accident. I guess I can understand checking his thermos for alcohol. That would make sense, but GHB? Who suggested checking for that?"

"I did."

"Really? That seems odd to me. Why?"

"I don't know. I just had a hunch. We'd just busted Longboard Johnson and your lady over there popped up on his Rolodex."

"So you zoomed right in on Mrs. Capella from the get go, did you? That's very interesting. Did you bother to send the coffee sample to an independent lab to have your results double-checked?"

"No."

"You'll agree that we're discussing yet another important piece of evidence, would you not? In fact, the *only* piece of real evidence you have to this day?"

"True."

"Then tell me this. You knew Mr. Aguilar was known to be furious with Mr. Capella, and to have threatened his life. Did you question him at all?"

"No."

"How come? Did you have a hunch he wasn't involved?"

JT's sarcasm wasn't lost on McCormick. He ran his hand over what remained of his white hair and pushed his steel-rimmed cheaters back up from halfway down his nose before answering. His face reddened noticeably. But he kept his composure.

"Simple. Motive? Maybe. Opportunity? Not so much."

"I see. Of course, that's assuming that the drug was in Mr. Capella's thermos when he left home. Did you ever consider the possibility that it was introduced after that? There must be a dozen or more cameras between his house and the accident site. Did you ever check them?"

McCormick said, "Mr. Holliday, I believe you've been watching too much true crime TV. This was a simple case. Open and shut."

JT said, "I see." He turned away as if he was finished, then spun back around and said, "One more thing detective. I wanted to ask Sheriff Reyes personally about it, but he refused to testify and my request for a subpoena was denied. Maybe you can help me."

McCormick said, "I'll see what I can do."

"You may remember that two years ago there was quite a scandal involving your department..."

Tanaka was waiting for it. He immediately jumped from his chair and shouted, "Objection, your honor. It's obvious where Mr. Holliday is going. This line of questioning is totally irrelevant."

JT shot back, "Your honor, this entire case hangs on one slender thread, the GHB in the victim's coffee. The central question is a simple one. Can we trust the Orange County Sheriff's Department's integrity or competence? A woman's life is in the balance. I believe we must have that discussion."

Judge Russo agreed. She said, "I'll allow it. But be careful Mr. Holliday. You are pushing the envelope. I'll be listening carefully."

JT said, "Thank you your honor." He turned again to the witness and said, "So it seems the OC Register broke the story after an extensive investigation. It wasn't pretty. There were forced confessions, beatings, faked lab tests, suborned perjury, you name it. Oh yes, and one presumed suicide by hanging. You recall that, detective?"

"Of course. It was a disaster."

"Indeed it was. On top of everything else dozens of convictions were overturned and the cases had to be either dismissed or retried."

"Yes."

"You were there of course, as a senior member of the Sheriff's staff. Can you tell us what steps were taken to remedy the problem?"

"Very strongly worded memos went out. Entirely new guidelines and procedures were adopted."

"Detective, Mr. Brad Johnson would have been a key witness in this trial. His legal situation was desperate. And yet your department neglected to place him on suicide watch. Is that an example of your new procedures?"

Tanaka objected that JT was badgering the witness and was sustained.

JT said, "Sorry your honor, I withdraw the question. But forgive me, detective, it strikes me that new procedures are fine but the real problem was with people. You had people who were lying and doing other dishonest things. They knew what they were doing was wrong. They didn't care. Guidelines don't fix that. Better people do. Can you tell me how many people in the department were replaced?"

"To my knowledge, no one was replaced."

"So, in the wake of this terrible scandal, no one was held accountable? No heads rolled?"

"Well, no, if you put it that way. No heads rolled."

"I'm by God putting it that way, detective. What other way is there to put it?"

Tanaka objected once again, but JT said, "I withdraw the question, your honor. I'm done with the witness."

* * *

Holliday's witness list originally had consisted of nine names, but since the trial commenced he was able to trim it to five. He'd wanted to make sure the jury heard the ME admit that no drugs had been found in Capella's system, but as Tanaka had already called said gentleman he was able to get that in on cross. He also had planned to call Ms. Gilliam to testify that Frank's children were next in line for the insurance money, but of course was able to expose that fact by way, once more, of his cross-examination of Roger Capella.

He wanted to put Sheriff Reyes on the stand, wanted it badly, but Reyes, being of sound mind, refused to play and Judge Russo declined to subpoena him. McCormick was a serviceable proxy, but JT had to soft pedal it a bit due to his age and reputation. Still, he was satisfied he'd made his point.

Finally, he'd briefly toyed with the idea of putting an expert on the stand from the UCLA School of Pharmacology to discuss the characteristics of GHB, but in the end decided it was too wonky and would just confuse the jury, not to mention carried the risk of actually cutting against us. You never know with experts.

And so that left five: the estate attorney who set up the Capellas' prenup and who could verify Delilah's account of its details, Archie Fenner for a first person account of the accident and the preceding moments, Dr. Scott for a brief discussion of vehicle dynamics, myself to discuss my investigation with regard to Lourdes Perez and Brad Johnson, and of course, last but a long, long way from least, Delilah Capella. Her testimony, of course, was the centerpiece of the affair, the scene everyone looked forward to, the event that would mark the moment of decision.

The estate attorney was first up, and was asked to recite the specifics of Delilah's arrangement. His version comported exactly with hers. When Frank died she was seven months away from a million dollars USD, free and clear of any strings, at which point if she was through with the guy she would have been free to divorce him.

Of course, Abi immediately realized the weakness in this argument. After all, a million is nice but it isn't as nice as five. And Frank's death relieved her of all that messiness that comes with a divorce. I could see the wheels turning in his head from where I sat. In the end, he made the smart choice to leave it for his cross with Del, or his closing argument.

Next up was my teacher and friend, Trevor, who due to his exceptional tutorial abilities was able to make the jury understand the notion of oversteer and instill an appreciation of just how twitchy and dangerous a Porsche Carrera can be. It wasn't like you had to be drugged to kill yourself in one of these contraptions.

Tanaka challenged him briefly with Capella's professional race training and reputation as a skilled driver. But Trevor brought the house down when he said, "Sir, there are a certain few activities that, when one engages in, one accepts the fact that no matter how skilled one may be, one may die. Yes, it's a small number, and I speak of pursuits that most people only read about. Flying fighter jets off an aircraft carrier comes to mind. Climbing Himalayan mountain peaks, maybe. Milking venomous snakes or training and feeding tigers, perhaps. I can assure you that driving high performance unstable automobiles at breakneck speed along a winding highway above a cliff qualifies for inclusion. Mr. Capella would certainly not be the most skilled driver ever to lose his life driving Porsche Carrera Turbos, I promise you."

Archie Fenner recounted his memory of Frank's crash, which agreed in every detail with what he'd described to me when I interviewed him. Then JT asked him the one and only question he was on the stand to answer.

He said, "Mr. Fenner, how long before Mr. Capella's vehicle departed the highway were you able to hear it?"

"That's a loud automobile, the Turbo. I'd say at least forty-five seconds to a minute."

"During which Mr. Capella was successfully following a winding road at high speed, all the while controlling his throttle and working his gearshift?"

"Right."

"Until suddenly, in one split second, you heard the engine quit or drop to idle and you saw him flying off the edge?"

"Yep. It was darn weird, I'll tell you."

"Does that seem like someone driving under the influence of a drug to you, Mr. Fenner?"

Abi objected to JT leading the witness, or asking the witness to draw a conclusion I forget which, and was sustained. JT had made his point nonetheless.

On cross Abi asked just one question. He said, "Mr. Fenner please tell us what time the crash occurred, as accurately as you can."

Archie answered, "I can give it to you pretty close. I was keeping an eye on my watch because my wife wakes at seven every morning and I wanted to start back home no later than ten to. That Porsche came flying at me between 6:40 and 6:45."

I was next up. JT first asked me, "Mr. Brennan, would you tell the court your occupation?"

I said, "I am a licensed private investigator. I was retained by the Pacific Life Insurance Company to investigate the circumstances of Francis Capella's death."

"And, in the service of full disclosure, you have a personal connection to this case as well, correct?"

"Yes, I believe that's pretty well known at this point."

"You recently had occasion to travel to Puerto Vallarta, Mexico, did you not?"

"Yes."

"What was your purpose?"

"I wanted to speak with Marcelo Aguilar's ex-wife, Angelina. I believed, and still believe, that it's possible he had a hand in Mr. Capella's death and I wanted to ask her thoughts about that. It was a loose end that I felt needed to be tied up if possible, and Pacific Life agreed."

"Did Mrs. Aguilar tell you anything of interest?"

"Yes she did. In the course of our conversation it emerged that the Capella's housekeeper, Lourdes Perez, is actually Mrs. Aguilar's aunt. Ms. Perez accompanied her to California as her chaperon when she married Mr. Aguilar. During the entire course of the marriage Ms. Perez lived in the Aguilar home. After the divorce Mrs. Aguilar asked Francis Capella, who had represented her, to hire Ms. Perez as his housekeeper. It was a personal favor."

Of course, at this point Tanaka went ballistic. He said, "Your honor, this is outrageous. This information was never disclosed to us during pretrial discovery. I demand that it be excluded."

JT said, "Your honor, we've only just recently received this information ourselves. Had the prosecutor done a thorough investigation he and the Sheriff could easily have developed it for themselves. This is just another example of their rush to judgment. They dismissed any possibility of Mr. Aguilar or Ms. Perez being involved from day one."

Judge Russo said, "Gentlemen, I will see you both in my chambers. This trial is in recess. Bailiff, please escort the jury from the courtroom."

JT later told me what happened in the judge's chambers. After a very heated argument she said, "Mr. Tanaka, Mr. Holliday has a point. You had every opportunity to investigate the housekeeper. Frankly, I find this line of inquiry interesting and obviously relevant. I'm going to allow it. I want to see where it goes."

Once the trial resumed JT continued his examination. He said, "Did Mrs. Aguilar offer you any insight into Lourdes's behavior?"

I said, "She told me that after Mr. Capella's death Lourdes was terrified that she might be charged. She said her aunt was desperate to get out of the country, but needed money. For years she had been completely dependent on Mr. Aguilar for her support. She told me that while she didn't know for a certainty, she believed it entirely possible that her ex-husband induced her to plant the GHB. She said that he certainly seemed as anxious to get Lourdes out of the country as Lourdes herself was anxious to leave."

If you've noticed that my testimony may have played a little fast and loose with the facts, congratulations. I reckon all's fair in love and murder trials.

144

Abi objected on the grounds that this was all hearsay. Judge Russo agreed and instructed the jury to disregard that portion of my testimony.

JT moved on to the subject of Longboard. He said, "Mr. Brennan, you also had occasion to visit with Mr. Brad Johnson while he was in custody, and very shortly before his unfortunate death. What if anything did he tell you with regard to his alleged role in supplying the defendant with GHB?"

"He swore to me that he had done no such thing. He said that the defendant's statement that she met him at the club to discuss his legal problems and her husband's possible assistance was absolutely correct."

Once again Abi raised an objection based on hearsay, but the judge said, "In this case I am going to let it stand. It's not the defense's fault that Mr. Johnson is no longer able to speak for himself."

With that, I was excused.

When Delilah was called to the stand the atmosphere in the courtroom was electric. This was the big moment everybody was waiting for. This was the ballgame, and everybody knew it.

JT started with, "Mrs. Capella, would you please describe for the court the circumstances under which you met your late husband?"

Delilah said, "Yes. I was fairly new to California and still trying to get my feet under me and determine a direction for my life. I was taking business classes at Orange Coast Community College, and Frank was teaching a class in business law that I was enrolled in."

"At the time he was a famous figure in Orange County. Were you impressed with his wealth?"

"No, not really. I grew up in Iowa, in a small farming community. My father was pastor of the Lutheran church there. We lived simple lives. I don't mean to sound naïve, or judgmental, but in Iowa we were not as concerned with money or social status as people are here. It was more about whether you were considered to be living a good life and were right with our Savior."

"Well, then, what was it that drew you to him?"

"At first I wasn't attracted to him in any way. Our age difference was a problem for me. But I guess I was impressed with his success. They say women are attracted to powerful men, and I suppose that was part of it. Still, it took a long time for him to win me over. He was very persistent.

In time I came to see that he was a kind man, and an old-fashioned gentleman. You know, a hold-the-door-open for you and send you flowers gentleman. And he was so much more mature than the men my age that I'd met. I gradually fell in love with him."

"I gather then that once you married your life must have changed dramatically?"

"The biggest difference was that I found myself living in a beautiful luxurious home. It was like nothing I'd ever imagined."

"Were you on the house's title with him?"

"No. He put that in his will for his children. He offered to add a codicil stipulating that if he predeceased me I would be given the right to occupy it as long as I wished before it passed to them. I declined the offer, as I had and have no interest in living alone in such a large home."

"I see. Speaking of his children, we have seen that they regarded you as a gold digger who was taking advantage of their father."

"Yes, unfortunately they did, as did his associates and their wives. They all pretty much ostracized me."

"They also claim that you forbade them from visiting your house. Is that true?"

"No, not at all. That was their decision. They pretty much cut me and their father out of their lives."

"How did your husband feel about that?"

"It hurt and disappointed him deeply. He used to talk about it. He loved them and understood they were sticking up for their mother, but he used to say it was fine for them to honor her but he was the one supporting them with his money and that should earn him equal respect. He said he worked hard for that and had every right to be happy."

"Tell me, was he generous to you?"

"Absolutely. He provided me with a Black Card with no limit for my personal use, and told me to spend as I wished."

"Did you spend lavishly on yourself, then? Jewelry, furs, designer clothes, expensive shoes, spa treatments, lunches with the girls at trendy restaurants?"

"Hah. That's not me. I'm not much for jewelry. Frank gave me this amazing engagement ring that must have cost him a fortune. For our first anniversary he gave me the diamond earrings I'm wearing. Last year he bought me a beautiful ladies' Rolex watch. Oh, and a couple of years ago he gave me a pearl necklace with matching earrings. That's my entire collection. I own no furs. I have never been to a spa. I have no girlfriends, nor do I enjoy expensive restaurants. I loved to cook for myself and my husband, at home."

"So what would you estimate your monthly expenditures on your credit card may have run?"

"I did spend perhaps $2000 a month on clothing. That was because Frank insisted. He always said my appearance reflected upon him and his practice and so I needed to look 'smashing' whenever we went out. His words. I was also in charge of keeping his wine collection up to date and provisioning our kitchen. He was a gourmet and a serious oenophile, always insisted on French wine exclusively, so with food that ran maybe three thousand a month. And of course I had miscellaneous expenses, like gas and maintenance on my car. The rest of the housing costs, the housekeeper and landscapers, the utilities and all, were paid by his accountant. I would guess that when it all added up it would have been no more than eight thousand dollars a month."

JT said, "You are a good guesser, Mrs. Capella. I have here, and offer to the court as defense exhibit A, the statements for your Visa card going back to the day you were married. The charges average less than one hundred thousand dollars per year. If you *are* a gold digger, you're a damned poor one."

Tanaka was not liking what he was hearing. He started to rise from his seat and offer an objection, but thought better of it.

JT said, "Mrs. Capella, I have one final question for you. It's a delicate subject for you, I understand, but forgive me, it must be addressed. The prosecution has theorized that a part of your motivation for arranging your husband's accident was the fact that he was a well-known philanderer. Do you care to comment?"

Delilah said, "Certainly. To begin with, my husband's sexual exploits were greatly exaggerated. He enjoyed the reputation for some reason, and believed it served to promote his career. But it's true that he was on occasion unfaithful to me. I finally had to accept that. I assure you it was a problem

147

for me. He was publicly humiliating me. I confronted him about it and gave him an ultimatum. I made it clear to him that if he didn't change I would leave him immediately, his money be damned.

"But I was raised as a Christian woman. I believed that as his wife I had a duty to do everything in my power to preserve our marriage and honor my vows to him. I was required to offer him forgiveness. He swore to me he would change, and when he died we were well on our way to healing and reconciliation. We made love for the first time in months the night before he passed."

JT said, "Thank you, Mrs. Capella. I appreciate your candor. Your honor, the defense rests."

It was clear to me that Del had acquitted herself very well. Her sincerity was undeniable. Now there was just one last act to this little passion play, Abi Tanaka's cross-examination. There was one last moment of peril for Del to survive.

It was surprisingly brief. Tanaka had only three questions, and as it turned out he never laid a hand on her. As with JT, he obviously recognized that there was little profit in making a woman appear sympathetic by beating up on her.

Abi said, "Mrs. Capella, as you know the subject of your housekeeper, Ms. Perez, has recently come up. May I ask if she lived with you full time?"

"She worked and lived in the house Mondays through Fridays."

"So she wouldn't have been in the house the Sunday morning of your husband's death, nor the day before?"

"That's correct."

"Thank you. So Mrs. Capella, your attorney has made much of the fact that your husband's death deprived you of the one million dollars your prenuptial agreement would have provided in just seven short months. But isn't that a very worthwhile trade off when compared to an insurance award of five million dollars?"

Delilah said, "Mr. Tanaka, after my husband's death, and before all this with my being accused of murdering him, I had decided to move back to my home town and move in with my father. He's aging, of course, and could use my company. Five million dollars is more than I could ever spend in Iowa. Life there, as I've testified, is simple and money goes a lot further than here in California.

"My attorney has advised me that in the event of my acquittal it's un-likely any other individual would ever be prosecuted and so my husband's death would have to be considered accidental, and the full five million dollars would be paid out. I feel I am entitled to the one million of that that I was guaranteed. As for the rest, I do not care to profit from my husband's death. I don't need it or want it, and I'm sure God has other plans for it. This morning I directed my attorney to advise the insurance company that four million dollars of my husband's insurance proceeds should be used to create an endowment fund in my husband's name for the benefit of St. Jude Children's hospital."

That really sucked the air out of the room, and was a real body blow for Abi to absorb. Nevertheless he quickly recovered and resumed his cross. He said, "That's very commendable, Mrs. Capella. Of course talk is one thing, actions are another. Promises made on the witness stand are easily forgotten after this trial is over. The jury can hardly be expected to trust them or consider them more than a convenient maneuver to enhance your credibility."

JT could have objected to these remarks, which were clearly out of line in the context of a witness cross-examination, but he decided to let it ride and allow Delilah to respond.

"Mr. Tanaka, excuse me. The jury may make of my testimony what they will. I am a Christian woman. God is witness to my words."

"So you say. At any rate, I have just one last question. Your attorney has proposed a theory that your husband made a stop somewhere or met someone after he left your house, and it was then that the GHB was somehow introduced into his coffee. Yet in your statement to the police after the accident you said that Mr. Capella left the house at sunrise. You just heard Mr. Fenner testify that the accident occurred between 6:40 AM and 6:45 AM. Sunrise that morning was 6:18. We checked. Obviously that would have left no time for a stop along the way. What do you say to that?"

"Mr. Tanaka, I say that you should reread my statement. I said that my husband left sometime shortly after daybreak, or I may have said first light. By that I meant civil twilight, which begins well before sunrise, almost an hour before. I can't say for sure that he left right at the beginning. It was probably fifteen or twenty minutes later. But he left well before sunrise."

Abi said, "No further questions."

Touché. With that Delilah had navigated the last dangerous waters and emerged unscathed. It was over. I was certain we were going to win this thing.

CHAPTER 33
THE TRIAL: CLOSING ARGUMENTS

This time Holliday was first up. He had arranged to have an easel placed in front of the bench, with poster board bearing the words *Reasonable Doubt* in large block letters. He pointed to it as he began his closing argument.

He said, "Ladies and gentlemen, two small words. Reasonable doubt. Two words that are the very foundation of our magnificent justice system. No one in this great country of ours, not you, not me, and not the defendant, can be deprived of liberty without proof beyond a reasonable doubt that they deserve such a fate. And I am here to tell you that in my entire long legal career I have never encountered a case that was as replete with reasonable doubt as this one.

"The prosecution's case hangs on the slenderest of threads, a coffee thermos purportedly tainted with Gamma Hydroxybutyrate. This is the only piece of real evidence presented to you in two and a half weeks. Imagine that, a murder trial with one piece of evidence. It's extraordinary. And so much doubt attached to it.

"Was there in fact ever any GHB in that thermos? Did the county lab technicians get it wrong, either because of incompetence or, worse yet, mischief? We don't know, but we can say that if they did, it wouldn't be the first time. This is why better police departments everywhere send critical evidence out to independent labs for verification. Of course, in this case that wasn't done, and so we will never know for sure.

"We have no evidence to prove that even if Mr. Capella's coffee was tainted, he ever actually consumed it. The medical examiner was unable to determine if GHB was present in his system. Mr. Fenner's testimony would indicate that prior to his crash Mr. Capella was certainly not driving like a man who was drugged.

"And then there is the question of whether, if present, it was introduced before or after Mr. Capella left his home. The prosecution, of course, wants to convince you that the only possibility is that it was placed by the defendant. I'm sorry, but that is far from certain.

"There are two people I so dearly wish I could have called to the stand for you. The first is Mr. Brad Johnson. Were he able to speak he would swear to you that he did not provide the defendant with drugs of any type. Unfortunately, thanks to yet another example of the Sheriff Office's negligence, he is no longer with us. He ended his own life rather than lie to save his own skin. Of course, you saw the Club Neon video, which was intended to bolster the prosecution's case but in fact failed to show the one thing they needed: proof of their allegation that an exchange occurred between Mr. Johnson and the defendant. Thus they only managed to create more doubt, more reasonable doubt.

"The second is Lourdes Perez, the Capella's housekeeper. Obviously, she had as much opportunity to spike that thermos as the defendant. She could easily have placed GHB in the bottom of the thermos days in advance. Would the defendant have ever noticed when she later poured her husband's coffee? I think that very unlikely. And we now know that she had a connection with Marcelo Aguilar, a man who had threatened Mr. Capella's life but was never even interviewed by the county investigators. What would she say if forced to testify? We will never know, as she has fled into hiding in Mexico. But we know this: her involvement fosters yet more doubt, reasonable doubt.

"And now I move to the last question of reasonable doubt. Was the drug, if it ever existed, introduced *after* Mr. Capella left his house? I will be the first to admit that when I first took this case on I found it very difficult to believe that someone had managed to pull that off. I would have agreed wholeheartedly with Mr. Tanaka's opening statement. I could not conceive of how that might have been accomplished. I tossed and turned over it. Then one night it hit me. It could have been what investigators refer to as a honey trap.

"Any one of the dozens of men who had cause to wish Mr. Capella dead could have enlisted an attractive woman to approach him, either by means of social media or perhaps in person at a bar, and lure him into a sexual tryst or tempt him with the prospect of one. It would then have been child's play to set up a brief meeting with him that Sunday morning, maybe for the purpose of arranging a meeting later that afternoon or evening to have sex. It could have been at this meeting that GHB was surreptitiously introduced. Mr. Capella's Sunday morning drives were well known, and the timeline as well as we can determine has more than enough ambiguity to allow for such a stop. It appears that there could be as much as thirty minutes of unaccounted time.

"Can I say with certainty that this is what happened, let alone prove it? Of course not, but neither can the prosecution prove that it wasn't. Their investigators could have reviewed footage from the many cameras installed along the victim's route of travel that fateful day, but they were too locked in on the defendant's guilt to consider any other possibilities.

"And so, once more, we are left with doubt, reasonable doubt. We are left with any number of individuals who had the opportunity to commit this crime, if in fact there has even been a crime.

"There are any number as well who had motive, of course. The list could extend for years into the past; after all, revenge is a dish best eaten cold. But I put it to you that my client is not one of them. You've heard testimony that confirms she was just a few short months from receiving a gift of one million dollars from her husband. At that point she would have been free to divorce Mr. Capella, if in fact she wished to be free of him. It's common knowledge in the legal community that prenuptial agreements are made to be broken, especially where flagrant philandering is involved, and so she could almost certainly have won a further generous settlement.

"Ladies and gentlemen, the defendant is a God-fearing Christian woman who has led a completely unblemished life. Believe me, if she'd ever had so much as a jaywalking ticket the prosecution would have found it and you would have heard about it. You've heard testimony attesting to the simple life she lived during her marriage despite having unlimited money at her disposal. Yet you are being asked to believe that she suddenly transformed into a master criminal and murdered a man she loved, all for a few more dollars she doesn't want or need and is planning to give away.

"Before you pass judgement on my client, I ask you to take a moment and reflect upon what this poor woman has been through. As you've heard, she grew up in a small farming community in the state of Iowa, a community steeped in quite a different ethos than you and I are familiar with, one of faith and simple living. When she was barely out of her teens she came here, to Orange County, to pursue the California dream. She was a naïve, unsophisticated young girl, but one with a solid moral grounding.

"She soon fell in love with and married a man of great wealth and power. She suddenly had access to almost unlimited luxury, yet she clung to her roots and declined to succumb to its temptations. She lived as close to modest a life as would have been possible in view of her circumstances.

"She was a loyal and faithful wife, yet her marriage eventually faced serious problems. Her husband proved to be unfaithful, and very publicly so. Where many women would have filed for divorce, Delilah fell back upon her Christian training and forgave him, urging him to work with her on reconciling and renewing their marriage. They were making serious progress on this process.

"Tragically, on the very eve of success, her husband died under tragic circumstances. This of course was a horrible twist of fate for her to endure. Yet worse was yet to come. She'd not even had the opportunity to grieve before she found herself wrongly accused by a Sheriff's Office and Prosecuting Attorney, with little or no real investigation and despite an almost complete lack of evidence and the availability of more likely suspects.

"Yet there was still worse to come and more pain for her to endure. She found herself being vilified by the lurid coverage of the press. She was dubbed the 'Black Widow.' Horrible and completely unsubstantiated things were printed about her. She could hardly recognize the woman they were portraying with their irresponsible reporting.

"Imagine, ladies and gentlemen, finding yourselves in this position. Please find some small modicum of charity in your hearts for this poor woman, I beseech you.

"You know, it's common wisdom that the accused in a murder trial should never take the witness stand. It's considered too dangerous to expose oneself to the cross-examination of a skilled prosecutor. Believe me, Mr. Tanaka is a skilled prosecutor. Yet my client did take the stand. She looked you all in the eye and told you her story, a story that has not changed in the slightest detail since the beginning of this nightmare. There were no inconsistencies for the prosecutor to attack. Her sincerity was obvious throughout her testimony and is clearly beyond question. Her innocence is the one thing, the only thing in this case, that is beyond doubt.

"Now it is time for you to render your decision. I understand what a formidable task you face. Fortunately you have one simple principle to guide you, one candle to light your path. Reasonable doubt, ladies and gentlemen. Reasonable doubt, the sacred underpinning of this process we call a trial. My God, we are immersed in it. We see it everywhere we look. You know what our system of justice requires. You know what the right outcome is. You know what you must do. I am confident that you will do it. Thank you."

* * *

So it came down to Abi Tanaka's closing argument. His words were the last that the jurors would hear before beginning their deliberations. They were remarkably brief.

He said, "Ladies and gentlemen, at the outset of this trial I suggested to you that this was a very simple case. Now, after two and one half weeks of testimony, this is what it remains.

"I will grant you that Mr. Holliday has provided us with a number of Byzantine theories and accusations intended to distract us from the facts. Without exception, they are fantasies.

"His notion of honey traps, with mysterious women and secret meetings, are particularly entertaining, but let's face it, they are ridiculous. I believe Mr. McCormick may be right. Mr. Holliday may be watching too much television.

"He has sullied the name of one of our most respected citizens, Marcelo Aguilar, a man of impeccable reputation. Mr. Aguilar believed that Francis Capella had taken the most precious person in his life away from him, compounding the offense by taking advantage of Angelina's fragile emotional state to seduce her for his own gratification. It's completely understandable that he might have said in a moment of anger that he'd like to kill Mr. Capella. I would have said the same and I believe any husband would have said the same under the circumstances. He obviously didn't mean it literally.

"His allegation that Lourdes Perez was desperate for money to flee to Mexico, and therefore induced by Mr. Aguilar to poison Mr. Capella's coffee makes no sense. Mr. Holliday himself has revealed to us that Lourdes was Mrs. Aguilar's aunt. In fact she was Angelina's only aunt, and Angelina was her only niece. The fact is that the two enjoyed a mother-daughter level relationship. If Lourdes needed cash she obviously could have turned to her niece. Angelina received an extremely generous settlement in her divorce and lived in a multimillion-dollar home in one of the most luxurious developments in Mexico. Clearly she had the resources to help with whatever her aunt might have needed.

"As for Mr. Holliday's suggestion that Mr. Capella may not have ingested any of the coffee, well, please. Common sense tells us that he didn't take a thermos full of coffee and not drink any of it. In the twenty minutes or so that it took him to drive to the crash site, he surely would have consumed at least a cup's worth. It's plain as day what happened. The drug began to gradually take effect in an insidious manner, causing him to slowly become drowsy. He misjudged his speed as he approached that fateful tight turn and reacted too slowly. He backed off the throttle but had no time to brake before he plunged to his horrific death.

"I must tell you that I take particular umbrage at the disgraceful manner in which Mr. Holliday has attacked the Orange County Sheriff's Office. These are hardworking, honest public servants who dedicate their lives to the protection of the county's citizens and enforcement of the law. They deserve better.

"Mr. Holliday alleges that the Sheriff's officers hounded Brad Johnson to his death. The fact is that Mr. Johnson was going to be convicted of raping a number of young women, many of them underage. He was facing at least a decade of imprisonment regardless of any testimony he may have offered on our behalf. That prospect would have been intolerable to a man accustomed to the 'Longboard' lifestyle he'd enjoyed for years.

"So now we turn to the one and only person who by any stretch of the imagination could possibly have been responsible for this death, Delilah Capella. There simply is no plausible alternative to that simple fact. She alone had motive and she alone had opportunity.

"It's all very well that up until this point she had lived her life as a good Christian woman. But even people of faith sometimes reach the end of their string. She was being privately and publicly humiliated by her husband's flagrant disregard for his marriage vows. This situation had continued for years, probably the entirety of their marriage. Clearly her appeals to him were going unheeded. She faced another seven months of his abuse if she were to salvage any of the money she'd been promised, and then a messy, contentious and further embarrassing divorce. There was also the fact that her husband was perhaps the most skilled family law attorney in the county, if not the state, and it would be anyone's guess whether or not their prenuptial agreement would stand.

"During her testimony she referred to her preference for living a simple life, and her plan to return home and enjoy a pastoral existence in her native Iowa. If that was really her intent, she didn't need even one million dollars. She could have just left without further ceremony and allowed her husband to keep his money. No, the money was important to her and since it was, it was all the better that the amount would be five million rather than one.

"I caution you not to be misled by her last minute offer to create an endowment for charity. This cynical ploy is a demonstration of her desperation, not an indication of innocence. It's an empty, unenforceable promise easily abandoned at her convenience.

"This crime was really the perfect solution to a situation she found increasingly unacceptable, and would have been the perfect murder except for the miraculous fact that Mr. Capella's thermos was ejected from his car and was not, as she anticipated, destroyed in the fiery inferno that claimed his life. It's strange, in a way, but I recall that during her testimony we heard the defendant speak of God's plan. It occurs to me that perhaps she was right. Perhaps He did have a plan after all.

"Ladies and gentlemen, we've come to the end of very long trial. I appreciate your attention and your patience. I lost count of how many times Mr. Holliday used the word *reasonable* in his closing argument, but in was quite a few. Well, reason is in fact what this is all about. And reason will tell you, if you use your own God-given common sense, one simple thing. The Orange County Sheriff's Office did not murder Francis Capella. Nor did Marcelo Aguilar or any other of Mr. Capella's aggrieved legal adversaries. Nor did Lourdes Perez.

"Delilah Capella and Delilah Capella alone committed this crime. She is guilty beyond any reasonable doubt. I ask you to hold her accountable. Thank you."

And there it was. The trial of the century ended and jury deliberation commenced.

CHAPTER 34
THE VERDICT

Years of court watching have taught me one thing: God help you if you find your fate lying in the hands of an American jury. The record is replete with cases of the egregiously guilty set free and the obviously innocent hauled off to prison. There is no way to predict what a "jury of peers" will do, no matter the expensive voodoo science dedicated to their selection. You may as well gut a chicken and read its entrails.

It took four days, but the jury in this case finally came back with a verdict in the matter of the State of California v. Delilah Anne Capella: Guilty. Murder One. JT's defense, as brilliant as it was, had fallen on deaf ears. The pretrial publicity had simply poisoned the jury pool beyond reasonable repair. Her fate was sealed before the trial had even begun. Delilah was sentenced to twenty years to life, with the possibility of parole after ten.

The hedgehog had prevailed. Abi had his scalp. We rolled the dice when we decided to refuse the plea deal, and the dice came up snake eyes.

Holliday was of course shocked beyond belief, as were the majority of observers who possessed any degree of legal training. Going into jury deliberation we'd been certain Delilah would be acquitted. Ironically, Judge Theresa Russo later revealed in an interview with the OC Register that had it been a bench trial, that is a trial without jurors, she would have acquitted.

When we got together, though, the three of us the next day, Del was surprisingly calm. Somehow, probably by virtue of her faith, she'd summoned up an inner stoicism. You had to give it to her; she was one tough little girl.

JT tried hard to reassure her. Worst case, she would still be a young woman when she was finally released. And he was extremely optimistic about the odds of a successful appeal. To his credit, he never bailed on her.

The appeal would rest on the refusal to move the trial to a different venue, due to the brutal manner in which the press had treated Delilah. Ms. Russo had run a good clean trial, and actually given his defense great latitude, so he could find no judicial errors to cite.

Of course, I made all the right noises for Del, assuring her of my undying love and my continued support. It was important for her to have hope of a better future, and for me to keep alive the possibility of resuming our romance upon her release.

I can tell you that when I left her that day, I felt really awful about how things had worked out and the unintended role I had played in the whole nightmare.

That was the last time I ever saw her.

CHAPTER 35
ERIK NORDSTROM REDUX

After I left Delilah, I had one more small errand. I needed to see my old buddy Erik Nordstrom. After leaving the jail I headed straight down to Irvine to his office.

He was in a meeting when I arrived at the Metatronics campus, and I cooled my heels for nearly an hour in the lobby before his secretary ushered me into his presence. I was beginning to believe this was a standard and calculated practice.

We shook hands across his huge desk, and after the usual pleasantries I reached into my briefcase and removed the engine control module I'd boosted from Capella's Turbo.

I held up the charred and dented box in his direction and said "Know what this is, Erik?"

He said, "I haven't the slightest idea. What is it?"

"It's the engine control module from a 2014 Porsche Turbo. Frank Capella's 2014 911 Turbo, to be precise."

"I'll be damned."

"Maybe so. The crazy thing is, there's this little tiny wire wrapped around it, see? Looks like copper. Looks like it snakes its way into the box and, I don't know, maybe hooks up with the mother board that carries all those amazing chips. It's been fused into the aluminum housing by the heat of the fire. I damn near missed it."

He reached for it but I pulled it back. "It's not supposed to be there, the wire. I've checked. So I'm asking myself, what the hell is that for, and I think, who better to ask than my old friend Erik Nordstrom of Metatronics, who of course knows all about computer chips."

"Did you now? Why would you be troubling yourself with this case

160

anymore, anyway? The police have their killer, and your company's set to slip off the hook. You have a nice payday coming, right?"

"I'm maybe not convinced the police have the right person. But about this control box. It occurred to me, maybe it's an antenna, the wire. I've always been puzzled about the way they said the engine noise stopped, just for a moment, before Capella lost control, and how the poor guy got so unlucky as to have that happen at the exact spot where the guard rail was down. Everybody told me Archie, the witness on the beach, was wrong. But I wasn't sure. His story kept nagging at me. So when I saw this copper strand, it occurred to me that maybe somebody was able to mess with his engine by radio control. Maybe somebody was able to shut his engine down at precisely the right time and induce a fatal case of oversteer, causing the poor guy to slide right off the road and into glory."

"No kidding. That's a hell of a theory. Any way to prove it?"

"Well, of course I don't have the resources to reverse engineer the chips inside, but I imagine the great state of California does."

"Which still wouldn't tell us who switched it into his vehicle, if that's what you're suggesting."

"True. You know, though…it's a funny thing. I stopped by and made a real nuisance of myself down at Newport Auto Center, just for shits and giggles, you know, and I learned there's a mechanic used to work there whose spending habits have changed markedly these past few months. He's only recently left the state, as it happens. He gave everybody some happy horseshit story about his mom winning the lottery, but that little yarn doesn't check out. He's the same mechanic who by coincidence performed a thorough checkup on the accident vehicle. Young kid, you have to wonder how he'd do under police interrogation. Johnny. Johnny Z I think it was. Ring any bells?"

Nordstrom isn't rattled by this line of attack. He's used to negotiating multimillion dollar business deals.

"The people who wanted Capella dead…that's not a small club, my friend."

"Of course you're right. I'm actually surprised they didn't have a parade when he bought it. Speaking of clubs, though, if we can get back on point for a moment, I wouldn't be able to estimate how big a club the people with competence to modify computer chips is; perhaps you have some thoughts on the subject.

"But you know, there's one more funny thing. I was exploring the hillside above the curve where Capella lost it, and there really is only one place that is both secluded and yet has a clear view of the road. Nice little spot just off the trail, lots of big boulders to sit on if somebody wanted to, you know, lie in wait. I noticed someone had done just that. There was a neat little pile of cigarette butts. Marlboro Reds. That's your brand, isn't it, Erik?"

He laughs. "Come on Brennan. Me and about a zillion other people. Number one seller in the world."

"Right. Well, God bless our tobacco industry, I do believe they're unfairly maligned. Number one in the world, as you say. Big help on the trade balance. Anyway, who knows after all this time if there'd be fingerprints or maybe dried saliva with DNA on them, the butts I collected. That's something the authorities would have to look into, I guess, if I decided to turn them over."

To which we have a few moments of silence, and then, "You work for the insurance company, right? Don't you make out better now that Delilah's been convicted?"

"Good question. The answer is a bit complicated. To the company, it doesn't matter, just so long as someone is. For me, it really would have worked either way but I actually could make out better if someone else was guilty. We've become close, the two of us. I'm her only lifeline at this point and she's invested quite a bit of faith in me, God bless her. I'm not one to tell tales out of school, but we were actually, um, intimate, before they hauled her away. I really would have hit the jackpot if she'd been acquitted. Especially if I were then able to identify the true killer.

"I was thinking we had a decent shot at that, until the Sheriff's people dug that video up, with her and Brad Johnson, the nosy bastards. That was sort of a bummer, actually. Anyway, I'm pretty sure that if she could get her conviction reversed on appeal, I could still have her. Her and her two and a half million dollars that she would then be eligible to collect. Or possibly five, depending on how much of a fuss the insurance company would decide to put up about the GHB."

Another moment of silence, and then, "But you're not looking to do that, else you wouldn't be standing in my office. Why not?"

I said, "You really are a smart man. I don't wonder you have a billion dollars. You're right, the way things have developed that's no longer the way to play it. I fear I'd get tired of her, beautiful as she is. To be honest, I'm really not a monogamous sort of guy. You know what they say, no woman so sweet that there's not some man out there who's tired of making love to her. Or worse, she could get bored with me. Her affection is, after all, trauma-induced, I suspect. Plus the money isn't in my name.

"Anyway, even five million isn't really sufficient to do what I'm looking for. That's why my number one priority is to ensure that you get away with it, Erik. That's the only way I can really get what I'm looking for."

"Oh yeah? What are you looking for?"

"I'm looking to retire, Erik. To a life of absolute luxury and debauchery."

"How much you figure a project like that would take?"

"I figure twenty-five million."

"That's a lot of money."

"Well, it is and it isn't. To me, sure, it's a ton of dough. To a guy like you, with your net worth, it's a rounding error. To a guy doing, say, life in prison, where the only thing to spend money on is cigarettes and Vaseline, hell, it's a fortune."

"So tell me this. Why were you so sure she didn't do it? What about the GHB?"

"Oh, that. I planted that."

"You have to be kidding. Why would you do that?"

"Just a whim, I guess. I found the thermos near the wreckage. The police missed it. There were still a few sips of coffee left in it. It occurred to me that in light of Brad's lifestyle and his connection to Delilah, it might work out to my benefit if it was doctored. I was thinking that if nothing else panned out at least I'd always have the bonus money, you know, for coming up with the one piece of evidence that really nailed her. Once we fell in love that changed everything, of course. But I couldn't turn back the clock. Now I needed to find a likely suspect to blame, or at least to appear to be trying. Lourdes was my best bet, perfect really, with her access to the house. Motive was an issue, but then I was able to connect her to Marcelo

Aguilar, who conveniently had publicly threated Capella's life. Problem is she has gone to ground. She's just evaporated. Nobody can find her. It was a real tangled mess I'd created for myself until you came along and presented me with an even better play."

"You are really one sick bastard, Brennan. What a wicked game you've been playing."

"I never killed anybody, my friend. Of course, if you refuse to see the light and I have to take this chip to the authorities the first question they'll ask is what about the GHB? I'd be forced to fess up and lose my PI license and most likely Delilah as well. I mean, I would have to spin one hell of a tale to walk that back for her, right? But of the two of us you have much more to lose. You aren't looking to do life no parole for murder one, are you Erik, what with you being a smart guy with so much to live for?"

At this point he walked over to the bar behind his desk and poured himself a couple fingers of very expensive single malt. He sat down, leaned back in his chair and spun it away from me and just stared at the wall for perhaps five minutes. Then he spun back in my direction. "So how does a numbered account in the Cayman Islands sound?"

Epiphany is really a beautiful thing. "Delightful."

"Good. Come back in three days. I'll have it arranged."

"Excellent," I said, and turned to the door. "By the way. It really doesn't matter, but I'm curious. Why'd you do it?"

"Because I could. Because he made me look foolish, and I can't afford to be made to look foolish. Three days, Brennan. And don't forget the fucking box, okay?" he said after me.

"Don't worry, pal. It's burning a hole in my pocket. Accessory after the fact has a nasty ring to it."

I carried the photo of Delilah in my breast pocket that day, and when I was out in the parking lot I pulled it out and took a quick look. It made me sad. It really was too bad about that Club Neon surveillance videotape. Before that surfaced I was looking like hitting the trifecta. I could have had Delilah, her money and Nordstrom's money. But that all paled, after all, compared to the effect it had on Del, the poor foolish girl. Oh well, one really needs to look at situations like this philosophically. Some days you eat the bear; some days the bear eats you.

Like I said, I feel very bad about the way things worked out for her. That's on the one hand. On the other…I really needed to move on.

I had a bit of unfinished business with Marcelo Aguilar. And I had a plane to catch. Aeromexico 334. Los Angeles to Puerto Vallarta.

If you enjoyed reading
WICKED GAME,
please leave a review to recommend it to other readers.

Made in the USA
Las Vegas, NV
11 December 2022

61783838R00095